T0114916

Cock Pit

A.V.A Treks

BALBOA.PRESS
A DIVISION OF HAY HOUSE

Balboa Press books may be ordered through booksellers or by contacting:

Balboa Press
A Division of Hay House
1663 Liberty Drive
Bloomington, IN 47403
www.balboapress.com
844-682-1282

Print information available on the last page.

ISBN: 979-8-7652-4876-8 (sc)
ISBN: 979-8-7652-4875-1 (e)

Library of Congress Control Number: 2024900097

Balboa Press rev. date: 01/29/2024

Chapter 1

My bicycle tires slide in the snow. The falling flakes grow larger with the darkening sky. The back streets of Amsterdam are hushed in the crystallized squall. Cobblestones sleep undisturbed, in winter's white. The populace has emptied the sprawling labyrinth of lanes and canals. They are having supper. I smell the warm roasts wafting out of doorways, taste the juicy gravies, and feel the glow of each hearth. Out alone, I am under a spell in the foreboding quiet. If there was someone to talk to, it would be compelling to whisper. I feel an exciting urgency, as twilight creeps around me. The city favors a windless secret. The black velvet cover of after-hours slides over me, like the locket cover of an ancient timepiece.

Tranquility embraces me as my bicycle wobbles over quaint bridges, and past identical cathedrals. I have no idea of my whereabouts, nor do I care. The map is useless because every frozen canal seems to be in triplicate. Each row of Dutch architecture is reminiscent of the last. The streets swirl in circles on islands. I float among them, surrendering whimsy to guide my slender, rented tires. I shyly slip unnoticed into the entrails of the ambiguity, and duck unknowingly through the backdoor.

Magical red lights glow through the blustery snowflakes, and I wonder at my cryptic passage. This peace I have found is the calm before the storm. The row of crimson lanterns light the foreboding answer. My gaze falls upon a lady of the evening. She is illuminated in the window, like a porcelain doll on a shelf. Peddling past more private portals, I try not to look. I am also too shy to look into the swinger's clubs, but the stone fountain sculpture of male genitalia is intriguing. I almost fall off my two-wheeled transport upon sighting the Erotica Museum. The entrance is guarded by a mannequin, also on a bicycle. The electrically enhanced dummy is pumping up and down while peddling, onto a dildo that's strapped to her seat.

My transportation to the red-light district wasn't just a rented bicycle. I flew a Boeing 747 from Chicago earlier in the day, although it was midnight when I left. As a pilot for a cargo airline, Solar Air, I fly about 17 days a month, to countries all over the world. I try to stay humble, a trait my father exemplified, but it's difficult to say "I fly a 747" without sounding arrogant.

Only three of us pilots at Solar Air are women, out of about four hundred crewmembers. By crewmember, I am also referring to the flight engineers. They sit behind the pilots, and their chair swivels sideways facing a panel overflowing with bells, whistles, switches, and breakers. They guard the intricacies of the engines. All are licensed mechanics who oversee fuel, hydraulics, electrical systems, and help troubleshoot during emergencies.

We pilots are rated by the Federal Aviation Association to fly the B-747 as captain. However, two captains on the same plane is considered a hazard, as our egos can be larger than the airplane. So it is by seniority date that we bid for the captain seat. During each flight, or leg, one pilot flies and the other handles navigation, radios, callouts, and ass-kissing. The role of flying/non-flying pilot then switches for the next leg. This is how airline cockpits are managed all over the world.

Lounging in the crew hotel bar, waiting for my co-workers to join me for dinner, I warm up with a glass of the Dutch national liquor, Jenever. I lean on a copper embellished chair overlooking the tree-lined canal. Dormant branches stretch to the empty air, offering only a chill in return. I'm not optimistic about the evening. Would my cohorts rather buy prostitutes in the red light district, than hang out with me? I don't have anything against that scene, but what is there for me? Women from all races and creeds are willing to perform any illicit fantasy men request. That's not fun for me. I try to live and let live, but I wonder how those women can sleep. I'm definitely not interested in going to any of the famous sex shows. Not with these coworkers anyway. I'm about to turn 30 years old, but my crew is at least 20 years older than me.

On the leg from Chicago O'Hare to Amsterdam Schiphol, I flew with Captain Pryon. Funny, easygoing, intelligent, and well-meaning, he is mostly bald, with residual white hair. His ebony scrub brush mustache gives away his hair's original color before it was leeched by years of pressurized cockpits, and tough times. His wife died two years ago when she fell asleep with a lit cigarette, presumably drunk. Their home burned down with her in it. Pryon was gone flying a trip at the time.

He is generally agreed, to be most likely to get busted blowing above blood alcohol levels on a random check before a flight, and spend six months in rehab.

Pryon arrives in a flurry of B-52s. Wherever we drink, he begins each session with a round of the Kahlua/ Bailey's/ Grand Marnier shots. His curious brown eyes search for mine and I'm caught unaware of the eye fucking, until it's too late. "You know, Ava, I think we'd be really good together. Why not forget about going out, and come up to my room". He voices it so lightly, that it sounds like a mild joke. Yet I feel him probing my soul with his intrusive gaze, checking the odds.

"That's really flattering, but I don't sleep with people I work with" I lie. Well, not really, I don't mean to sleep with people I work with. But I do slip up occasionally when they con me. My intentions are always to have a long-term relationship. My intentions are sometimes stomped on.

I don't ever want anyone to feel like less of a person, so I continue, "I really like you as a friend and co-worker. I'm sure you'll have no problem finding romance here."

I regain my footing and hope he won't resent me from now on. It seems unfair because I should have the right to not sleep with him without retaliation. Life has shown me otherwise. However, I don't consider it sexual harassment. I try to view it as a compliment because he wants me, and is just trying to find a resolution to his feelings. My father used to say, "If someone is mean to you, you should feel sorry for them." My father taught me compassion. When people are offensive, that helps me to cope.

My father was a fighter pilot, and my mother was a nun. Mom left the convent after 14 years, with just the clothes on her back and a few dollars they gave her. Her career continued as a teacher, but I feel sorry for her students. My mother was one of the meanest people I've ever met. The type with a wooden ruler that stings your backside, and sarcastic criticisms that hurt even more. That's why I ran away from home.

My thoughts return to the noisy bar room of cigar smoke and foreign languages. Of course, I forgive Pryon for blatantly asking for sex. But does he really think I'm that easy? I'm nothing special, just an average American girl- brown hair, green eyes, and a little taller than most. My arms and legs are too long for my size, making me feel like a gangly teenager. When I'm off work, I'm very laid back. I try to treat people the way I wish they'd treat me.

But I feel more at home in the air. In the air, I'm hyper-tuned to the aircraft and sensitive to the engine's operating parameters. Although I am a licensed aircraft mechanic, I much prefer flying. The view is better. For a long time, I thought anyone could fly, and didn't understand it's a skill some people are born with. Other useful traits include reacting quickly during emergencies, and I'm always looking ahead. As a child, I was accused of not paying attention. Actually, I'd already lived the moment and moved on. Luckily, that type of situational awareness is a desirable attribute for flying.

Our flight engineer, Rouse, joins us swigging his obligatory B-52 and ordering a Southern Comfort chaser.

His voice is squeaky, "You guys get enough sleep today?" Rouse is looking at my legs as if he's wondering are there panties under my short black skirt.

Rouse is a repulsive pervert, disguised as a sweet, old man. His slight figure and glasses are enough camouflage to fool people, other than those who fly with him for more than one leg. I have flown many legs with him. Rouse is a married man, with a hooker in every port. He calls them "girlfriends" when he brags about his exploits.

"I got a nap." Pryon replies "You ready for dinner and some window shopping?" he teases Rouse.

"I just want to do some innocent peeping" lies Rouse.

Pryon also knows he's lying. "There's a terrific Argentine steak house around the corner" his eyebrows raise, "Are you coming with us, Ava?"

"Sure, I'm in," I reply. I love a good steak, and why not tag along for humorous companionship? I'm also a little curious about what happens here after midnight.

After midnight, the trolls emerge. The enchanting spell that hypnotized me earlier, shatters like an heirloom vase. Serenity is replaced by floods of international tourists looking for a free show, or cheap lay. Hustlers and hookers swamp the gothic bullpens of ill-repute. Working girls are stuffed into every nook and cranny, and the competition is fierce. There is every shape, size, and color imaginable. This is definitely the distasteful end of the food chain, and it smells rotten.

"That one looks like someone's ex-wife" Pryon exclaims about an angry-looking woman in a window. Her cropped blond hair bares impressive muscles on her mostly naked body. I wonder if she has children at home she needs to support. I'm relieved when he says, "Let's hop into that pub across the canal"

Momentarily, we escape the horde of whores. However, it doesn't take long for my fellow travelers to become concerned; and myself overjoyed. After another round of B-52s, we realize we're surrounded by about fifty men, and my crew wants to leave. They nervously whisper that we must have mistakenly landed in a gay bar, and I am laughing. It is oh-dark-thirty in the red light district, what woman in her right mind would be here?

At last, I found pleasure- I'm the center of attention. I mingle freely and gain confidence. I smugly confirm with the bartender, while acquiring our next round. He assures me we are definitely not in a homosexual establishment. Not many women venture into the red light district and the working women stay in their cribs. Lucky me.

My coworkers aren't convinced. Back on the streets, we trip the red lights fantastic. Again I am gratified, and awestruck. Down one of the seedy alleys, unexpectedly I see men in the windows. A huge sign on the stone building proclaims "cock rings". I jump with glee and feel like Susan B. Anthony when she was allowed to vote. It's not that I would ever buy a man and his treats. It's just that there are equal rights. I can have my cake and eat him too, same as the men. In my dazzled shock I blurt out, "Are you guys for me?"

Pleasure becomes pain, as one fancy dancer replies "Not for you honey", with a twirl of his limp wrist. I cringe in horror. It's all an illusion. My homophobic associates are literally running now. I fear becoming lost in the dilapidated back streets alone, so I lope after them, my spike heels catching in between cobblestones, waving goodbye to the cheery queers.

Back down the heterosexual haunts, the army of trolls overflow into the gutters like a torrent of human bile. Occasionally I am blasted by the scent of cannabis floating from a coffee house. Rouse is preoccupied, and as I approach him I can see why. The most beautiful Latino girl is in the window in front of him. Her face is elegant, in a striking, ethnic way. She looks like an Amazon warrior, yet she is young. How can she be old enough to decide that sex with strangers is her life's work? I sense she is trying to look indifferent, but there's something innocent about her. Her coffee-colored skin blends with waist-long, chestnut hair. She looks exotic as if she just stepped out of a rainforest. A beauty mark is strategically placed under her left eye. Her eyes are green like mine. Is that why she seems intriguing?

"I'll catch up with you guys later." Rouse is finally choosing a "date" for the night, and he slinks off into the shadows. I secretly hope it's not the young girl with green eyes. I can't imagine how horrible that would be, to sleep with a man like Rouse. I mean ugly on the inside. Someone with no morals, who doesn't care about the health and welfare of others. I don't judge the topless women in the windows. I'm all about people having the freedom to do what they want in life. I just feel sorry for whoever has to give themselves to Rouse.

Pryon and I duck into another hole in the wall and I am overjoyed to find a freckled woman with strawberry blond curls. "Where are the other local women?" I ask her, "Why are you the only one here?"

"I'm just out with male friends tonight.' Unfortunately, her Dutch accent is defensive. "I usually go to bars in other parts of the city"

I try to show her, I'm harmless. "I'm with co-workers too. If you don't mind me asking, how is your love life affected, living here?"

"Living here is helpful. The non-committal men are obvious. I'm free to find one sincerely looking for a relationship because if he just wants sex he can buy it anywhere."

I appreciate her bluntness. Inspired, I flirt with a few strapping gentlemen at the bar. Some have Irish accents. Luckily, I don't have to worry about Pryon feeling thwarted. He easily befriends a crew from Speedbird Airlines, also on layover.

I feel attracted to a dark-haired, stocky guy, and wonder how his whiskers would feel on my face. I believe in love at first sight. It's only happened to me a few dozen times. His chiseled jaw is so perfect he's hard to look at. His potent blue eyes remind me of the deepest sea. A feeling of strength radiates from him. The strength mountain ranges are made of. He's not feeling shy. "I love how your earrings match your eyes."

I'm surprised by his words, because that's why I wore them. I'm also surprised by his American accent. "Where are you from?" I ask.

"Virginia Beach" He answers "I'm Steve" he says, extending his muscled hand. "I play the piccolo in a band, and I'm here training with my friends from Ireland."

"And Scotland." The ginger speaks up. "I play the bagpipes."

"Oh cool." I respond, shaking Steve's hand. "I'm Ava. One of my coworkers plays the bagpipes." I laugh as I tell them "We are cargo pilots. So it's very entertaining when my friend brings his bagpipes on a trip, to practice on the flight deck."

The guys look at me in disbelief and momentarily fire questions at me. Steve gathers me into his uniqueness. He's such a powerhouse. Who knew that musicians could be brawny Herculeans? The closer I get, the more inescapable he seems. His sexy voice strokes my mind, "What are you doing in here?" He's referring to the fact that I'm the only woman in this dive bar.

I do not hesitate, "I want an intimate relationship, with a nice guy. What better place to find that?" I respond jokingly, but we share a gaze of mutual enthrallment.

"Why would you want a relationship tying you down?" He's open to conversation at least, and interested in what I have to say.

"It's the simple things" I respond, "Waking up in someone's arms. Cooking breakfast together. Having someone to share life's beauty with."

Steve's intimately studying my expression, so I continue. "Last week I hiked up a mountain in New Zealand and watched the afternoon sun create rainbows across a waterfall. During moments like that, I always wish someone else was next to me, enjoying it with me. I always feel like I'm hogging it all to myself."

"I feel like hogging you to myself" His husky voice is in my ear, kissing my neck now. I feel relief surrendering to him. I revel in the discovery, alignment, well-being, and completeness. Like it's the right time, right place, right person. I appreciate his attention to me and it feels solid.

My biological clock has a five-alarm fire bell, and I don't have time to discuss the weather. No one seems to want to date a girl who is gone most of the month. They don't seem to trust that I would be faithful. But I really would. I would even give up my career for the right man. Something's missing in life, and I suspect it's having children and a real family. I don't want to end up depleted, like the wrinkled, 50-year-old flight attendants I see dancing in the Wan Chai bars of Hong Kong.

I sample his wet lips and make a confession. "My underlying fear used to be that I would die alone. Then I realized, I've been alone most of my life, so who cares if I die alone."

"I could die in your arms right now" he whispers, but the sound of breaking glass shatters our conversation.

The muscled musicians become an intelligent choice because Pryon and the Brits, have entered a bar brawl with some sweaty-looking radicals. Pryon knocks one of them down a flight of stairs to the basement door, warning us "They have knives".

The target of my affection, swings one of the instigators against the wall, and hammers away on him. I smile serenely. Do I know how to pick them? I feel as if the intrinsic forces of the universe orchestrated our meeting.

Sirens are closing in from the outside and everyone involved evacuates, jumping into taxis. My hero rushes me into a cab around the corner. Steve seems like such a nice guy, and he's so hot. I wish I could see him again. Luckily, he climbs right in. He has every quality I look for. He's funny, smart, protective, and intensely good-looking. I feel shielded in his embrace. I'm jubilant to be galloping through the streets with Prince Charming in my pumpkin taxicab, and it's way after midnight. His touch is soft and moves right through me. I want him so bad. I want to show him how good I can make him feel.

I wake up to hear my own voice yell "Wait". It sounds terrifying. The glaring numbers of the hotel's clock radio taunt me. They are oversized and painful to look at. They remind me of the red lights last night. I gingerly touch the sheets next to me. My arm overextends, stretching against the empty expanse of hard mattress. My lover has left.

My blurred vision sees past my blind heart, but it was exhilarating. Steve grabbed the top of my dress with both hands and literally ripped it in half down the front. He was all-encompassing. I love our chemistry and the way we are together. I thought we had mutual respect, but now I feel cheaper than a call girl. I deserve love, not the screeching halt of abandonment.

I don't know if I felt him leave, or if he left earlier, and I was somehow strangled until that moment when I awoke. The "Wait" came from my discarded subconscious; my expendable self. Everything stung and throbbed that he left me. I'm so naive for thinking we could have a future together. I was tricked by just another one-night stand.

I limp to the bathroom room and see his watch on the floor. I also realize $200 in Euros was stolen from my jacket during the bar fight. I say money doesn't matter, but it hurts almost as much as my sore body. I had plans for that cash at the Waterlooplein Market. I wonder how much the watch is worth. Maybe I can make back my $200. I need coffee and wanted to ice skate at the Rijksmuseum.

I move closer to the bathroom mirror. Any time someone insults me, or I feel like a victim, I compliment myself to balance it out. "I'm going to love my life, exactly as it is," I say to the abandoned plane wreck looking back at me. Maybe I don't need a relationship. I'm fine on my own and have plenty of fun. A few times I joined the mile-high club, although never at work. Not that I wasn't asked. I've climbed up airport beacons and had mind-blowing sex up there. I've lost my panties on runway numbers. I even made love inside the intake of an F-16. Yes, two people fit in there, you just have to be careful of the airspeed probe.

But I'm over it. I don't want to be single forever. I examine Steve's watch. It's a Lumonox; silver, with a black face. I wish it didn't dangle off my thin wrist. It has an inscription on the back, "Tank. Blue Team. May the bullets be high and the water be warm. Alaska Air Guard". What? We didn't even discuss Alaska. I know

Chinook helicopter pilots in the Air Guard, maybe they know him. I suddenly feel obligated to return his watch. But why? He left me. Why do guys have to be so messed up? Words are streaming into my head faster than I can write. I'll call it…Timeless.

When I woke up this morning
Could have guessed you'd be gone
Found your watch in the corner
Ticking at dawn
Did you leave in a hurry?
For what were you late?
Will you come back for your watch?
Will it help me wait?
Will it count off the time?
I waste looking for love
Will it count all the men?
I miss intimacy of
For they come and go
Somewhat like the time
As I seem to be falling
For each pick-up line
Can it tell me to stop?
Waiting your return
Can it tell me apart?
From each head you turn
Can it tell me how long,
For who, and what for?
Can it tell me what time
I should expect more

Chapter 2

My fingers deftly push test buttons and set dials. I flow through the overhead panel switches of my jumbo jet. My motions are automatic after years of repetition. Finally, my hands come to rest on my oxygen mask. After cleaning the rubber with an alcohol swab, I gratefully huff a bit to get the brain moving. Plus, a little extra to chase away last night.

After the usual scheduling mess and customs nightmare, we are finally launching in the evening. I run through my personal cheat sheet, making sure I remembered everything in my expanded flow preparing the jet. This includes reviewing our weights, critical fuel calculations, getting clearances, and testing the HF radios, I check the alternate airport minimum weather requirements, and the appropriate thrust settings and speeds for take-off.

Pryon finds a plastic leg from off a Barbie doll on his side of the cockpit. It was accidentally left there by a co-worker of ours, who carries it as a joke. He uses it to identify which pilot is flying, by saying "It's your leg" and handing it over to the other pilot. We get a good laugh together. We needed an icebreaker. It was all business in the lobby for pick-up, and I'm stuck in close quarters with him and Rouse for the next twelve hours.

I make a nest with the stuff I carry in my flight bag- pens, paperwork, calculator, and gum. I also carry a laptop, passport, ear plugs, sunglasses, small world atlas, list of country codes for making phone calls, a foreign language dictionary of survival phrases, scented lotion to revive with, and a notebook with tips I collect about each airport and each airplane. They all have idiosyncrasies since they are ex-passenger planes converted to freighters. This aircraft is set up with some switches, like the landing lights, working backward than the other planes.

I also keep a copy of the General Declaration (Gen Dec). I learned that the hard way. I accidentally had a pair of trick handcuffs in my flight bag going through Hong Kong. They were made of plastic and part of my homemade FAA Halloween costume. My crew and I had flown ourselves into China, but now we were commercialing out. Going through security my handcuffs were found and dangled on display by the strict-looking, Hong Kong officers. This discovery was to the joy of my normally grumpy captain. His Italian eyebrows raised in a moment of fleeting respect.

My flight engineer, who knew me too well, chuckled. They left and went to enjoy the First Class lounge. Then things got scary for me because security took my passport and called the airport police. I had no proof as to how I arrived in Hong Kong. This was a rookie mistake, and the only thing that saved me was my flight engineer eventually returned, wondering why I wasn't boarding with them at the gate. He had a copy of our Gen Dec.

Most pilots keep a book of gouges and charts to make things easier, such as electrical schematics, and international speed limits. One chart shows metric conversions of feet, so when the Russians clear you to 10,400 meters you can look at the chart and know you are cleared to flight level 340. In layman's terms, that's 34,000ft. I also carry an attitude of naive optimism. Maybe because no matter what I step in, I usually come out for the better. I try to create my own reality. Feeling as happy as possible, and project that into my future plans. Or it could just be dumb luck. Too bad that luck doesn't bleed over into my love life.

I load our destination and waypoints into the ship's computer. OMDB, The International Civil Aviation Organization code for Dubai, United Arab Emirates. Pryon and I crosscheck our time, distance, and fuel. It's my leg, so Pryon is the non-flying pilot on this leg. He'll handle radios and navigation equipment, and track our positions on a plotting chart, through areas without ground-based navigational aids.

Rouse drops a stack of Hustler magazines on the floor next to the control pedestal. He queries "Is it normal for a woman to have chest hair?" I'm stunned by this question, and before I can reply, he continues "My new girlfriend in Amsterdam has a few. They are about a half-inch-long, black chest hairs. Just a few of them I mean. Have you ever seen that before?" Thank goodness Amsterdam Air Traffic Control interrupts him with our clearance.

"Solar 7391, cleared to Dubai via the Arnem 1V departure, as filed. Expect Flight level 370 within 10 minutes. Squawk 3369". I read back the clearance and crosscheck it to match the navigation we programmed in the ship's computer.

I brief the Departure, as the sun falls from the snow-laden clouds into the Atlantic. "Takeoff weight's at 734,100 lbs. It looks like we'll taxi down Yankee and Victor for Runway 01 Left. Flaps 20, 33 degrees assumed temperature, gives us 10% N1, and full climb thrust. Speeds are V1 151, VR 170, and V2 180, with a 400-foot stop margin. After takeoff, we'll fly heading 029 to 8,700 feet, per the departure procedure. If anything happens before 80 knots, we'll reject for major system malfunctions. If anything happens before V1 we only reject for fires, engine failures, or failure to fly. After that, we'll continue per the engine out procedure, follow the emergency checklist, and jettison fuel over the water if able, before returning. Any questions?"

"Did you calculate 'Here to Beer' time yet?" Rouse quips.

"Well, takeoff's at 1730 Zulu. With seven hours of flight time, plus clearing customs, finding our limo, and the half-hour ride to the hotel, I'd say nine hours, from here to beer. Figure in the time zones and that will be 4 am local"

"The only thing open then is the Hurricane Club," Rouse says. I briefly wonder where the Hurricane Club is. I don't think I've been there, but it's time for me to be a slam-click and ditch these guys.

Taxiing an aircraft that's 231 ft long, is done with a tiller. It feels like steering by Braille because it's challenging to see the taxiway line that's 29 feet below you. So you intuitively find your way, by straddling the light indentations on the taxiway centerline, with the pair of nose wheels. You try to stay on the taxiway centerline, yet not feel the thud of hitting the lights on it. To make a 90-degree turn, you roll past the taxiway's bend until you think your flight engineer is sitting on it, and then make the corner. "Radar, on. Engine ignition, flight start. Packs, off, no. 2 on. Autobrake, armed. Body gear steering, guard down. Caution panel, lights out. Landing lights, on. Before Takeoff checklist, complete"

"Solar 7391 Heavy, cleared for take-off Runway 01 Left".

We burn down the darkness of the runway. Patterned lights are reminiscent of the red light district, soon to be a distant memory. My rudder becomes more responsive from the effects of wind pressure at about 60 knots, like a willing stallion, my Pegasus rears up towards the sky. Pryon calls out our decision and safety speeds, "V1... Rotate". Now I'm past the point of no return, committed to gently pulling the yoke back, and pinning my airspeed on the dial even if we have an engine failure. I feel the G's pushing me back in the worn, beige fabric seat.

The remaining runway slips away and I call "Positive rate, gear up." The plane trembles and personal items shift, but that is on the periphery of my focus. I feel the firm controls respond to my grip, like the reins of a stallion, and feel relief, to be leaving behind millions of people in their city of vice. As the landing gear obediently tucks itself into our wheel wells, I pitch to 5 degrees and truly leave it all behind. I concentrate on proper speeds during flap retraction and fly precise headings and altitudes determined by the Amsterdam Departure procedure plates. Most pilots throw the autopilot on right away, but I like to hand fly until about 15,000 ft. We get so little stick time because, at high altitude, she's balanced delicately on a pinpoint of thin air. We fly trapped between the barber pole (overspeed) and the stick shaker (stall speed). A contributing factor, as to how high we can fly, is our weight. The 747 Classic, tops out at 833,000lbs.

"Autopilot comin' on" I announce the start of 6.5 hours of trying to stay awake. The Classic 747 doesn't have autothrottles and Rouse helps me monitor those when he's not asleep with his head on his worktable. Breathing is not to be taken lightly when your workplace is pressurized to 8,000 ft. The lack of fresh air dries your skin to parchment. Eyes that strain to see traffic against the sun, prematurely wrinkles the brow. The sucking sound of jet engines sucks your hearing away, sucks the moisture out of your body, and sucks the consistency from your life. Pilots miss seasonal changes, rhythms of day and night, flowers growing, and relationships progressing. Cargo planes like ours, are the worst on your body because the insulation's been ripped out to allow for more freight to be carried. There's also not much between us and the electromagnetic radiation. I hum a couple bars of "Rocket Man", to comfort the emotional separation from Earth, and normalcy. In my mind, I change the words to "Rocket Woman".

That awareness of being different is familiar to me. What secretly drives us, is the sensation of being part of a traveling, worldwide community. The ego trip of driving the largest passenger jet in the world. 90 million dollars worth of hot, vibrating, metal ecstasy, not including the freight. It's like being in a secret club called "Size Really Does Matter". The only people who truly understand us are other members, and they alone speak our secret language of techie terminology. EICAS, EFIS, INS, and ILS- the stuff that comes from years of mastering your profession, culminating in the FAA-type rating. Nothing beats arriving in your office with a front-row view of the sky that is yours, and knowing what to do, to own it. The illusion is of being elite, when at our core we know we're just glorified bus drivers.

My Dad warned me that airline jobs were boring. Flying with the autopilot on isn't really flying. It's sitting. He flew commercially for over thirty years, and I pretend his spirit is sitting out there on my wing. It's easy to picture him there, with a big smile across his face, kicked back in a relaxed pose. He just wasn't like these guys. I could swear he never cheated on my Mom. I have six brothers, and they don't seem like the cheating kind either. Ironically none of them fly. Half get airsick. When I was born, there had never been a female airline pilot. So I grew up thinking women weren't allowed to fly, but I lived in a fantasy world, where I could.

I'd arrange the household furniture into airplanes and put my little brother in "the back seat", teaching him to fly. I remember traveling on airliners and talking into one end of the seatbelt, pretending I was getting clearance from the air traffic controllers. My earliest memory, at about age three, was staring up at jets in the sky, thinking they were in heaven, and pilots were gods. Ironically, some really believe that about themselves, especially Captain Richard Cranium.

I was never given the model airplanes my brothers got to build, that I secretly hoped for. I was supposed to be the lady. A pink lady who minded manners and played with dolls. But I was a muddy mess, climbing trees with sap-matted hair. I was a disappointment. I was ignored and sometimes beaten. By age 13, I found my way out of depression by becoming a rebel. And so it was, I learned to fly, at the age of 15. In high school, I was staying out half the night in the Iron Hill Saloon & had fake ID's for buying the booze required to escape from my abusive home life. My dad gave me the usual lecture of a parent who realized they'd rejected their child for years and now it was too late, "Ava, what do you want to do with your life"?

"Since women can't fly, I guess I'll become a flight attendant."

Before you can say "Eating plastic food with a swinging lavatory door in your face", I was at the airport. Dad helped me pay for my Private Pilot's License. I made the decision to stop partying and fly instead, but Dad got Alzheimer's. I wasn't allowed to care for him, so I left, at age 17. That's when I graduated high school. My mother got rid of me early, at age four, by sending me to kindergarten before the age normally allowed. Now she smugly got rid of me again.

Life improved dramatically when I slept, ate, and breathed flying. I lived in hangars and when I wasn't flying scenic tours in spam cans, I apprenticed to be an aircraft mechanic, without pay. I swept hangar floors for dollars, washed planes, and took every ad hoc flying job I could. Working my way up, I eventually flew multi-engine aircraft like the beloved DC-3, hauling car parts out of the Detroit area. Because of my time flying old radial engines, and the maintenance experience, I was eventually hired to drop retardant on forest fires with aging Navy planes. Aerial firefighting was real flying. Planes with no autopilot, and lots of grunt work.

Hypnotized by the constellations over Europe, I drift into happy memories of fighting fire with Tanker 17. I can almost feel the humid, Washington air soaking into the dewy airfield. The blinding, morning light forms mandalas through the array of sprinkler systems in the apple orchards. "Smoke?" I hear the lead plane pilot blatantly dare. His blond good looks and porn-star mustache stare across the Columbia Gorge. It doesn't take long for reality to slide back out, from the eclipse of hope. It was simply a truck on a dirt road disturbing the dust. Back to telling "There I was stories", and doing whatever possible to amuse ourselves.

The fire bell actually rings. The hours of boredom are ending. I grab my guitar and run for the plane. Anything left behind may never be seen again. The Forest Service dispatchers could send us to Southern California for the rest of the season at any given moment, including once airborne. Most of what we own stays on the airplanes. Luckily, my P-2 Neptune has plenty of room for my mountain bike. The 1950s–era Navy sub–hunter is stripped of its radar and endowed with a firefighting retardant tank in the bomb bay.

"Scramble, scramble", the ground workers tease me as I hurry past. In the midsection of the plane, I open the manifold valves and muscle up the corroded toilet valves. Rightfully named, because a plumber designed this particular tank and used actual RV toilet valves. They cross-feed between the six "doors" available for selecting how much retardant to drop at a time, denoting coverage level. I yell to the slurry guys that it is safe to pump, and reassuringly smell the potent red stuff as I look down the vent/sight. There is also the slight scent of urine because the retardant tank doubles as the potty. If the urge hits in flight, you can put a padded toilet seat on its velcro mates atop the vent; bombs away. I slide into my Nomex flight suit and clumsy boots.

Watching the slurry bubble to the fill line, I give the ground handlers the cut signal out the window. I hear Captain Cobear climbing the front stairway and sliding the door closed. I leap over the tank and other sharp metal objects to strap into my humble right seat. My ears rejoice to the familiar "You want to start yours?"

Mine. Eighteen cylinders of pure bliss. I greedily turn the #2 fuel pump on low, crack the luscious throttle, and count the massive blades passing my window as I press the start toggle. Those beautiful paddle-blades that grasping for air, our lifeblood. The chance to truly live. After nine blades, I snap on the mag (make her hot). As she coughs and whirs, I change focus onto the RPM gauge and instinctively hit the primer toggle with my middle finger (make her wet), releasing the start toggle from my index finger. The smoke and vibration is thrilling. After she settles down, and I can keep her at an even RPM, I horse up the mixture control. Cobear already has the inverter on, so the AC gauges are working. I patiently watch him crank his engine. The rule is, if anyone backfires one on start-up, they have to buy the beer later. Unfortunately, I've heard that phrase a thousand times, and never actually got the beer.

We are headed to a small fire over flat land; boring. Although tougher for a lack of depth perception. Hilly terrain seems most erroneous, because it lacks a reference horizon. Still, nothing like Oregon the week before. We were every which way but inverted. The air was boiling. During the first drop, we pulled so many G's trying to pull out before smacking a mountain, the aft hatch busted open. Several drops required a sideways position along the ridge, and then the number one tank door wouldn't open. So after a "normal" drop, lucky me got to crawl into the hydraulics bay below and manually open the valve. I floated a little from my proximity to the sudden spewage of trapped fluid.

As we wait for the temps and pressures to come up, I busy myself flipping the switches of my office- oil cooler doors, radio, and nav selectors. It's Cobear's leg, and he taxis using a tiller on his sidewall. I test the control surfaces. The Neptune is unique because it has a varicam; the center panel of the elevator surface is hydraulic. We vibrate our way to the threshold of pleasure, as well as the runway.

Taking off in an airplane you haven't flown before is like losing your virginity. Testing those first moments of sensitivity, your lover comes to life in your hands. Leaving the ground in a warbird has the distinctive transition from vibrating like crazy on the ground, to a comparably gentle sensation in flight. The P-2 has two Wright 3350, prop-driven radial engines. Each contains 2,200 horses that lug around eighty gallons of oil per engine. It is also blessed with two J-34 jets, so ancient they burn the same fossils as the radials.

I line up the last important rituals as the captain lines us up on the centerline. Hatches closed, cowl flaps trail, mixtures rich, fuel pumps on; good to go. I give the radials a last, longing glance, and start throttling up the jets that really don't need to be babied. I announce "Jets up", although they do just fine announcing themselves, and feel Cobear release the brakes of the beast. We're off like a truculent turtle. My eyes scan the panel for needles dropping out of place and count off the airspeed in ten-knot increments so my co-worker doesn't have to look down from his take-off picture. During these first few critical moments of becoming airborne, I continue my diligent instrument scan. However, I am simultaneously aware of buzzing a friend's home, a few streets north of the airport. It makes me smile to think of the Navy Admiral, Roger Ball, who is probably smiling back up at me from his garden of antique cars.

Our Neptune is hot, heavy, and rocking with 22,050 lbs of red stuff, armed to drop immediately at the slightest emergency. The most famous jettison may be when a Circle-K convenience store was painted fuchsia by a Neptune that lost its engine after take off. That night, zealous smokejumpers snuck out to the flight line and plastered Circle-K bumper stickers all over that poor airplane.

Instinctively, I scan the engines for excessive oil or vibration, and verify the gear is up. We are struggling to climb above the Columbia River with not much in our way to the fire, besides other aircraft and restricted airspace. On arrival, we scope out the fire's boundaries and listen to the ground pounder. He attempts to describe where he wants the line of slurry, to the lead plane Bronco pilot. The Bronco scoots around finding the good and bad air, while choosing a route with great respect to the wind. In short order, a "show-me" is flown at higher altitude. Our lumbering Neptune obediently follows him on an invisible lease of loyalty. Our scrutinizing eyes are outside and inside; discerning and sometimes skeptical. On this hop, the jets, flaps, and other electric and hydraulic nuances are mine to befriend. I set them up for slow flight on approach, so we may drop at a speed close to stall. This maintains the falling slurry has more time to spread out, for maximum coverage area.

We draw lazy, red circles around the fiery, black scar. Liquid tourniquet to the angered patient. Sickly burnt earth, agitated by the slightest breeze upon its skin. Crackling and moaning in falling trees and dying life.

The smell of wood smoke has an odor-linked memory, like firing a weapon. At first, it seems vaguely familiar, and then recoils upon your mind with a riveting lucidity. We pull the trigger, dropping two doors at a time as advised by our leadplane. A P-3 joins us on the fire. Four years later, this same P-3's wings collapsed upwards during a drop, from structural failure of the center wing section. Never fly the "A" model of anything. Rest in peace.

Our mission on this fire is to protect a natural gas line. I love having a sense of purpose in my work. That's why I originally was inspired to become an aerial firefighter. "Load and return" commands the ground guy.

My soul is soaring through the canopy, but the lead plane pilot must have better things to do. "A few more ground crews could put this thing out". Cobear's lips drop cuss words, like chewing tobacco from a cowboy. However, he's a chain smoker so he lights one up, to enjoy on the return flight while I fly. Cobear uses a fuel selector valve as an ashtray.

"Your landing," Cobear announces. He likes to do all the take-offs, because they are critical when we're fully heavy. In exchange, he gifts me all the landings. Most people think that landing must be the hardest part, but I find it is the climax of my airborne romance. Intuition is finely tuned into this focal point, of wanting each landing to be the best I've ever made. Not for my co-workers or any onlookers. Just for me. Those last fragile, reactive moments are an apex. She settles in with my guidance, in a flurry of expander-tube brakes and power-recovery turbines.

The assistant tanker base manager is waving her magic wands, signaling us to familiar parking. She completes her tasks uncomplaining, despite her incurable, painful skin disease contracted during the first Gulf War. The Neptune and its oily ensemble, shakes to a standstill, like a puppy dispelling fleas. Dispatch released us. We worked ourselves out of a job again. Now I'll earn my pay with water hoses, washing the red and black stains from my heavy baby. I also enjoy pampering my sultry fire tamer with deserving sundries of oil and fuel. My aircraft mechanics license is useful in times of inevitable entropy. Especially that inevitable time called Winter.

The windsock flaps lazily with afternoon zephyrs. Shadows close like peaceful curtains, over the fertile Columbia Valley. Soon my bonfire will glow, and toasts will be made. I prefer camping, over having a hotel room. Some of my coworkers came to see my setup and liked it so much, they moved in. We gather for our nightly dinner party around the campfire. Before nodding off in my tent, I appreciate how lucky I am. I'm lucky to be flying Tanker 17 because I'm the only woman pilot doing aerial firefighting this summer. I'm also lucky to be alive, because gravity sucks.

Rolling down the runway
Blood pumping faster
Fabric wings leap to the sky
Of which I try to master

My heart clutches the feeble air
And strains to be the breeze
Tearing at the gravity
That brings me to my knees

It should be, we're self-sustained
By our own floating power
Disdain this mushroom earth of mud
Where lesser men just cower

But we throw our ships through clouds
Like dirty metal toys
Recklessly abandoned
By windswept pilot boys

Mechanics hands should shape-shift
Without a welding rod
Pilots should be airborne
Without the slightest nod

I know my will is stronger
Then physics and gray matter
And I won't fall from the sky
Like bird shit's gentle splatter

If I become the unfeathered cure
No man has dreamt thus far
I'd kiss you in a winged blur
And leave you as you are

Chapter 3

I dreamt of going to Rio De Janeiro my whole life, for the biggest party on earth. It's not random, that we are flying a 747 load of condoms into Rio for Carnaval.

"Ava, are you flying with us to Santiago tomorrow?" Our flight engineer is a biker. He is also a player. He's trying to maintain sexual relations only with his girlfriend, and his other girlfriend. He's also considered most likely to end up in a coma after his helmetless head bounces off a meridian.

"I was on days off, but the company needed me to fill in for your last pilot, who got sick." I explain, "I've always wanted to go to Rio, so of course I told scheduling I'd accept the trip. I also told them not to bother buying me a ticket home for a week. I can't believe I'm finally going to Carnaval."

"Do not leave your hotel room in Rio." Captain Cranium orders. The only thing bigger than Captain Cranium's ego is his wristwatch. I'd rather clip my toenails than listen to his snooze-inducing sermons. By takeoff I was already speculating, the pilot I'm replacing must have called in sick, just to escape from Cranium. Once he squeezes his over-inflated head into the cockpit, he disagrees with everything said.

"Why not?" I ask, pretending to care what he thinks since he's going to lecture me either way.

"Well, for one thing, it's the kidnapping capital of the world."

Actually the neighboring city, Sao Paulo, wins that title. But I'm not going to argue with the blowhard. Cranium continues, "I have a buddy who was mugged in Copacabana on his first day there. They just surrounded him and took his wallet, watch, and glasses." I am pretty sure they wouldn't be able to lift Cranium's watch.

Richard Cranium can't tell me what to do when I'm off duty. But since I have to operate this flight with him and we're only halfway to Rio, I play along, just to get him to shut up. "Our handler set me up with a really cheap studio apartment, a few blocks from Copacabana Beach. But if you say it's dangerous, I'll cancel."

His midwestern accent smacks of condescending bullshit, "By God, you'd better cancel. That city will eat you up and spit you out. The average Brazilian citizen has an income equivalent to $200 US dollars a month. They will rob you blind, to feed their family."

Time to give myself a break. I wasted most of my life being ordered around already. "I'm gonna go tap a kidney, and heat up my meal." I casually say, "Do you need anything?"

At least I can escape from him for a few minutes. Women weren't meant to sit still for ten hours straight in a cockpit, even if it was named after us. "Go ahead. I'll get up after a while," Cranium says, stretching his oxygen mask over his monstrous head. FAA rules dictate that when one pilot is left alone up front, they have to wear their mask in case of a rapid decompression.

The upper deck of the 747 is open, with a few rows of first-class seats remaining facing the galley. Since we haul mostly freight, we don't have flight attendants. While waiting for my food tray to heat up, I force my lethargic body to do push-ups. I nervously look under the seats, checking for snakes. We refueled in Manaus, Brazil and the locals were bragging about a twenty-four-foot Anaconda caught gliding down the taxiway. I remember hearing a loadmaster was bitten by a Cobra that hid in a pallet from India.

I try to be friendly to everyone, and treat everyone equally, whether they are a Captain or a Cleaner. Sometimes walking through airports, people mistakenly think I'm a flight attendant. My reply is always "No, I'm just the cleaning lady." That way I get a good laugh to myself, and I don't make them feel bad about their mistake. Often we carry a loadmaster and a mechanic on board the plane. Those guys sleep in flight and work while on the ground. They just ride the plane and never get off. It must be a disorientating lifestyle.

My loadmaster approaches from the cargo hold, "Hey Ava, come check this out."

I am numbed when he opens the plane's maintenance storage closet, to display illegal jaguar furs. He's so excited, "Do you know what these are worth?" All I can think is- Why is he showing me this? He had to display his illegal trafficking to someone? I could care less, I just hope our only stowaways are dead animals. Thankfully, the flight is almost over, so I can escape the crazy personalities on this trip. We start our descent, lowering ourselves into the horrid confines of gravity. Similar to wading into a septic tank.

Bleep bleep. Bleep bleep. The alarm in my rented Copacabana apartment wakes me at 11 pm, because I know when parties start. The shower has only cold water, but I'm hot again already. I received a flyer on the beach, about a local club. They throw the local soccer team's annual party, and it's tonight. I hurriedly dress in the red and black team shirt I picked up from one of the many street vendors, and I appreciate that my black mini-skirt matches everything.

Heading for the elevator, my stomach feels like fighter jets are performing aerobatics in there. I've never been to Rio, and hope I can muster a taxi. Before the rickety elevator can reach me, a lively black woman materializes from the apartment next door. A red bikini hugs her angular physique, and she sports red bows in her extended, ebony hair. I feel overdressed. Her three-inch heels have little red bows too. She looks at me and starts squealing with cheerleader joy. She is babbling in Portuguese.

I am flattered by her attention, as she sprays red glitter on what relatively little exposed skin I possess. Neither of us cares about the communication barrier. I am relieved to be adopted by such a friendly local, and she is overly happy to escort me to the dance. Her name is Louisa, and my intrepid vacation suddenly explodes, in a boom of fishnets and cosmetics.

Our taxi slows in heavy traffic and people barrage our windows. I don't know what they want. There's no street lights here, and they're screaming at us. I hear glass breaking in the distance and feel apprehensive. These locals are hostile. I'm so relieved Louisa knows what to do. Her daisy chain of blood-curdling profanity would make a convict cower. The mob moves on to the next cab stuck in traffic, and Louisa is nothing short of a bikini-clad, Amazonian angel.

Arriving at the club, there is another kind of mob scene. The entrance is clogged with tourists from all over the world because we have to purchase tickets from a heavily guarded kiosk. With my limited Portuguese and butchered Spanish, I would've never figured it out alone. We make it past the line of bouncers only to find the same situation inside for buying drinks. We buy tickets and then use them at the bar, although you have to yell to be heard above the live band. It's surprising how thirty or so musicians can crash out a tune with just brass horns. The bar is on the right, with levels of tables descending to a sunken dance floor on the left. Rising from that is the stage. Colored strobe lights swirl across the riot, like humanity in a cocktail blender. It smells like a locker room, with a splash of cherries.

Gulping my first of many Caipirinhas, an aggressive Latin thug assaults me. He humps my leg and tries to kiss me. His tongue is sticking out. Yuck. I'm petrified because I can bench press 100 pounds, but he's overpowering me. I can't push him away, although I try with all my might, and with worsening results. He's overpowering me and won't stop until he gets what he wants. I shriek for help above the sonic Brazilian music, but people just stare at us. Finally, I hear a guttural roar that actually makes the disgusting beast lessen his stranglehold. Louisa is saving me.

She bellows at the dog with such hostility, that he flees. I am definitely buying this girl drinks, all night long. Well, she needs me too. As the hours fly on, her bikini top flies off. Soon she is wearing nothing but glitter and her g-string, as are many of the women. The throng sways under the disco balls and conga lines break out like a heat rash. Louisa is warmed up now. She assumes control of an empty table and dances the samba faster than a Formula One Ferrari. Her wild gyrations are inspirational. Men gather at her feet and look like they're worshiping a holy, blessed Madonna. Except their eyes are bulged out and they're drooling. Some admirers try to stick their noses up her butt.

I kick back on the ledge behind Louisa, guarding her back while enjoying a front-row seat at the party. I feel sorry for all the men I know, who would kill to be in my spiked heels. I might not have learned the Samba so quickly, if not for Louisa. Dancing all night is brought to perfection in Rio. An art I am proud to collaborate on. If I don't tear my dress or lose jewelry, I don't feel triumphant in the morning. The number of mostly naked people on tables increases proportionately as time waltzes on. I stagger to the bar for another round. My buoyancy's swamped when a herd of Latin lovers surround me and pull up my miniskirt. My limited self-defense instincts take over, and I laughably flail some karate blocks in the air. They save face by stepping back and laughing at me. Little boys. Not getting my toys. I pull down my skirt sheepishly like a traitor because my undies are bright blue, not red or black.

I get our drinks and recover to the safety of Louisa's side. Balloons, streamers, and confetti float through frenzied yelps and funneled madness. The flood of humanity swells and surges with the class five rapid melodies. My shoes are trampled off as I'm smothered by the serpentine conga line. I have to do justice to the night. I owe it to myself to have a good time, but water isn't hydrating me and my ears are ringing. Two Scandinavians are yelling at me above the crowd's roar. They want photos of me with them. They think I'm Brazilian because of my tan and dark hair, so I explain I'm from Alaska. They don't care where I'm from, they just want photos. In between the camera crew and flying silly string, I realize they are leaving. Happily, they agree I can share a cab back to the hotel district. It sucks that I've lost an ear plug, or I would stay longer.

Their taxi pulls away from my apartment building and I hear, "Mamá, mamá, mamá" The eerie, monotone voice is amplified in the alley of high rises. It sounds like the cry of a stuffed baby doll, tainted with fear. "Mamá, mamá, mamá." A child of three or four years emerges, searching the ethereal realms with her wailing call. Straight coffee-coloured hair is tangled with grime. Looking into her dark, empty eyes, she has the thousand-mile stare of a trauma victim. Her bare feet are black with dirt, and her face is smudged. My feet are also bare and dirty. Finding my shoes was hopeless on the compressed dance floor.

The slender fingers of dawn clutch the road and its gray sameness. The pallor envelopes her, and I smell urine. The nearby ocean booms, over the white noise in my head. "Mamá, mamá, mamá." bleeds over it. My sore feet beg to lie down, and the unlit street makes me feel vulnerable. My fuzzy brain is a wasted burden, but I am haunted by her. Is she lost? Did someone leave her? Will they come back? Should I just mind my own business? "Dónde Está Mamá?" I whisper, turning my key in the apartment building entrance.

Stepping into the narrow corridor, I let her decide by offering "Vamos, Aquí." I'm aware my breath leaves a trail of decaying Brazilian Brandy. She scrambles inside, and then I sense relief. At the elevators I smile, confirming that she is ok now. I motion her to my apartment. It is simple but nice, about 25 ft long and 10 ft wide. I want to give her the bed, but she curls up in a corner. I place a pillow on the couch for myself and signal her to the bed. Cautiously I approach to check on her, but she is already asleep.

In the afternoon, I knock on Louisa's door, hoping she'll know what to do. I don't have anyone else to turn to. I just want to find the parents of this lost little girl and get her home. I don't know anything about children, and don't know what she eats. All I had to give her were power bars from the emergency stash in my luggage. She inhaled them like a vacuum.

Louisa's booming voice opens the door, with her usual, incomprehensible paragraphs. The sweet girl perks up. Louisa is so happy to see us both. I hardly know this woman, yet she treats me like an old friend. She hugs the little girl, "Gabriella", and hollers back into her apartment. A girl of about twelve emerges and embraces the little one. What a relief; they know her. The girls disappear into the backroom, and I stumble through the language barrier "Bebe en rua. Dónde está Mamá y Papá?" Louisa's eyes widen and then hollow, like empty tin cans. She whispers, "Gabriella, No madre. No padre." The normally boisterous woman seems to lose feeling, and visually shut down.

My brain can't register to compose another question. I flip through the language dictionary I brought along, at a loss to find the words I need. When I saw the older girl, I assumed she resembled her father, since she looked nothing like Louisa. The pre-teen was robust, with frizzy hair, and lighter skin. Now I realize she could be adopted also. A knock on the door interrupts my stunned stupor. A woman our age enters, with another young girl.

The little one runs in, curls bouncing, and shrieks when she hears the others. Louisa livens back up to her normal autobahn speed and introduces us. The older girl has brushed the knots out of Gabriella's hair. They tie ribbons around each other, gathered around an oval, antique mirror, while Louisa and her friend speak. Using my Portuguese dictionary, I ask Gabriella what she wants to be when she grows up, and am surprised when I find the translation. She wants to join the Army. I am grateful for the primping party. The little girls lovingly decorating each other in costumes, festooned with feathers. It's refreshing to spend time with other women, even if I can't understand 90% of what they say. Growing up with only brothers, I've found it challenging to bond with women. My girlfriends at home are other female pilots I've met in Alaska. Rarely are a few of us even together, off-work at the same time.

I gather with the girls in front of the mirror. Various religious trinkets & photos are pinned on the wall. I can't believe my eyes. There staring back from a crumpled photo, is the beautiful girl with green eyes…from Amsterdam. She has the birthmark on her left cheek. I know without a doubt, it is the same elegant, Latino girl I saw in the window of the red light district this winter.

I really wish I knew Portuguese, or at least better Spanish. "I know her" I blurt out. "I saw her last month in Amsterdam." Everyone goes quiet, with confused looks. Louisa takes me to the back room.

Through sign language and international women's intuition, Louisa conveys the girl's name is Monique. She's been missing for over a year. Everyone knows something terrible must have happened, because Monique was happy, and would never have just left. I sadly remember how beautiful she was. Undoubtedly at such a young age, she was grabbed by human traffickers, and sold into sex slavery.

My shared grief with Louisa becomes unbearable. I can do something. I know where she is. I describe the location, situation, and my own occupation. Louisa is in disbelieving awe, that I'm a "Pilotá". I vow to her that I will somehow bring Monique back to her. I'm not sure she believes me, but I am determined. I explain to her that there are groups of people who rescue kidnapped people.

I heard the Navy SEALs have a compound near my cottage in Alaska. I have a girlfriend, Mio, who goes there sometimes to use their hot tub. Didn't she say there was a group of them that rescues runaway teens before they end up in the drug dens and crack houses? She said they have rooms full of ski gear, bicycles, climbing gear, and every weapon imaginable.

Louisa hasn't told me what she does for work, but she must make a lot more than most people in Brazil. Her apartment is only a block away from Copacabana Beach. More of her friends show up, with more girls. But where are the boys? Don't any of them have sons? She gives me a T-shirt that says "Eu Quero E Mais'". She and her friends have the same shirt, and we put them on. She says we're going to a parade in Ipanema. I'm guessing the women made these shirts for their group to wear, and maybe that explains why I don't see any boyfriends or husbands.

The clouds smear themselves against the burning sun as we step into the street. It's like living in a blow dryer. They warn it can be dangerous near the parade, and the girls stay at the apartment. I'm wearing a concealed fanny pack, and toting a disposable camera. I never wear expensive jewelry anyway. My life in general, is fairly disposable. If I have anything nice, the hotel maids steal it.

We eat at a beachfront cafe, lined with palm trees. I love the swaying, tiled sidewalks and Samba music blasting from every street stall. After stuffing ourselves with fried meats and salad, we receive take-out bags for the leftovers. Getting up to leave, I notice everyone leaves their food bag behind on the table. Louisa sees my confusion, and motions for me to walk. A group of little boys is watching. They come over, chatting and laughing. I have no idea what is said, but they pick up the leftover food bags. These women are feeding the homeless boys. Why have I never thought of that? Why have I never seen it done before? People should be doing this everywhere.

My first view of Ipanema is thousands of people dancing. They are packed on the beachside promenade with bands, floats, and silly string flying through the air. Their ornamental costumes and make-up are seemingly oblivious to the afternoon rain shower dousing them. Everyone is hugging, singing, and spraying white foamy shit all over each other. Culture shock makes it very difficult to believe I'm here.

In Dubai, it's illegal to kiss or hold hands in public. In Rio people are humping half naked in the streets. It's honestly the most fun I think I've ever had. Riding the parade's current of hedonistic exhibition, I'm sucked into a medley of hysterical transvestites. The "girls" are whooping it up for their annual opportunity to bear it all. Their complex costumes have been painstakingly fabricated. I'm unavoidably propelled along, squished in between the fairy Oompah band and the gay Chinese dragon masquerade. The indulgent mosaic of gleeful queers, corkscrews up the boulevard, devouring it.

I find it thrilling to see their liberated sexual orientation. Some are dressed in Middle Eastern attire with peek-a-boo flaps over their genitals. Another is only covered by an elephant trunk puppet. Entangled in the wigs and make-up, I can appreciate them as bold and visionary. Their negligees are lavishly amplified. One creative "lady" wears a bra made of plastic baggies with straws protruding from the nipples. A fluid resembling apple juice is inside the plastic baggies. Thirsty? Not really. A large, hairy human of dark complexion, wears a braided, blond wig, fishnets, and the uniform of a traffic cop. She is standing in the road directing traffic. A distracted bus driver almost hits her. Unflinching, she toots her whistle. Cheers to the untethered, evolved ones, tonight they are truly free.

At the Sambadrome, a mile-long stadium, the decadent party rivals any other in the world. More than 30,000 locals spend the entire year creating songs, dances, and choreographed routines. They handcraft elaborate costumes and ride floats exceeding 30 feet high. That parade starts about 10 pm and lasts until after 7 am the next morning. I dance for the entire nine hours.

The simmering audience of about 90,000, sways through the dark hours, and bubbles to a boil just before dawn. Daylight breaks like the cracking of an egg. The rising yolk scrambles up the sky, spraying our faces with sticky, euphoric smiles. The sun is pouring gasoline over the fire of humankind, and we erupt into explosive celebration.

I don't know if there's singing in the street below, or if I still hear the music in my head. The following night. Louisa proceeds to dress me for going out. She doesn't like my work shoes, which is all I have left, so she gives me a pair of clear plastic high heels. Not borrow, give. She insists I wear silver, sequined shorts, but they ride clear up the crack of my ass. The clothes in Brazil are unlike any I have seen. I'd have more coverage from a strap-on dildo. She gives me a sequined satchel that matches the shorts, and a tight shirt with a giant blue butterfly on it. Louisa's equally undressed friends show up, and we go out.

Strutting the white and black tiled paths of Copacabana's beachfront, we are a demolition team for any man's heart. I could swear people are staring at us. We are a group of...No. I wipe the thought from my mind. The perception creeps back as the crowd parts and gawks in our wake. I am no longer a tourist. I am spellbound. With each swinging step, I sway bewitched into another lifestyle. I have the strangest sensation of being...a hooker in Rio.

Louisa is a hooker. We drift past the lines of mortals in the queue for the main doors at the "Club Mayday" Discoteca. We sail into a separate entrance, where the obligatory cover charge is waived. What have I done? Suddenly potential dance partners seem intimidating. I am no longer swimming after sharks. I'm retreating like a pearl into its oyster scum. I'm not a whore and don't want to be mistaken for one.

Jellyfish tentacles and colored searchlights hunt me out. Foaming fingers grope across my sequined sea bottom. Mermaids on pedestals perform for dirty pirates. Where is my mermaid? Louisa? She is wrapped in the algae of a scary stranger's arms. A wave of loneliness breaks upon my heart, its undercurrents slam my body with its undertow. The spinning dance floor swirls like the flushing of the gene pool. I'm being sucked under, by the continual caipirinhas I've sucked down. A clinging shrimp attempts bubbling communication. I snap shut like a clam. I go for the door.

I release the rejection I've been carrying, from men the world over. I slip the clear, spiked heels off my toughened feet and run as fast as I can through the filthy streets of sleeping homeless people. My bare feet clock out an even rhythm, that is thankfully soft. I run so swiftly, so silently, and so ecstatically, that no one can wake up quickly enough to assault me. There's an explosive pattern in my life, an emotional disguise of unfulfilled love that's been controlling me. It unravels with my lightning steps. Unleashed and unprotected, I disintegrate into my own echoing footfalls, leaving a void that must now be filled with unconditional love.

The first ray of a determined sun strikes the forgiving Christ image on the hill, the Corcovado. My arms spread as wide as the statue, embracing all of Rio. I witness the fluorescent ivory, burn the cobalt sky with divine intervention. Gasping in awe, I resurrect with the Redeemer and smile through my tears. I've been unknowingly adopted by hookers in Rio.

It's not only me they've adopted. Louisa and her friends are literally housing and feeding all the abandoned and homeless little girls. I vow to do everything I can to help them. Every child deserves a safe place away from molesters, criminals, and the mentally ill. Maybe I should start an orphanage, and retired prostitutes could run it. After all, Louisa can't do this forever, and she must be pushing forty. What do prostitutes do when they retire? The numbers race through my mind. The average citizen in Brazil makes only 200 US dollars a month, but the hookers make 50 bucks a customer. No wonder they can live in the high-rent areas, near the tourist hotels.

I am in awe that Louisa and her friends take care of so many children. I should be doing that. First I need to rescue Monique. I can't wait to get home and meet the local Seal's. They'll know what to do. I float into a fitful sleep. Eventually dreaming I'm a…Jet Queen.

I feel like a queen on a sunlit throne
Riding high above my home
My jester brings coffee, with a groan
I gaze out over the great land below
And smile serenely on the snow
Capped peaks. The world is my show
And I am free wherever I go
My million-dollar, silver-breasted chariot glows
And steers thru the air, effortlessly
Guided by satellite birds soaring free

In their own orbits and formations
Return my look, with the flicker of attentions
All is well this flight, my gleaming device
Obediently blinks, of alignments precise
Farmlands and gold-laced clouds
Medieval woods wrapped in alto-stratus shrouds
Not a whisper, on the outside
The sky is pleased, by this smooth ride
Satisfied I won't be late
Trust in my horsepower steadfast gait
Contrail breath in frosty air
Noble patience permeates your stare
Stars fall away in the light
As you are perfect in my sight
I really wish to see you again
But on your heart, that may depend
For I just fly, don't stop for long
It's just a way to pretend I'm strong
And hold myself up, to standards I've forged
Out of mirrors cast off, and broken swords
Don't you see? I would stop for you
The lover I had, a day ago —or two?
But no one's asking, and no one knows
When the ride will stop, and true life shows
Some meaning to the trivial woes
That ride the wind to where it blows
For now I'm only queen, high on this throne
Of cocktail parties, and midnight moans
The only life I've ever known
Is the lonely chosen path I've flown

Chapter 4

Inescapably, flying took me to Alaska. I delayed coming because I wasn't sure if I was a good enough pilot to survive. I am still unsure. I figured since there weren't many roads, it was the best place to fly. What I didn't know was the lack of roads meant a lack of places to refuel.

Remote airports, which are few and far between, make it just interesting enough to wish you were on the ground. I don't call myself a bush pilot, and I hate scud running. What I do love is ski flying. Chasing the Iditarod down the trail. Landing on a frozen river and listening to the frosty hiss of a musher's sled, floating by like an apparition. Landing on powder snow feels like sinking into a pillow. It's a tickling sensation accompanied by snowflakes spraying from the prop wash. Ice crystals burn the nostrils and taste like seltzer.

After 26 hours of commercial flights, I can't help but smile with relief as I drag my bag to my dilapidated doorstep. The snow banks are halfway to the roof, but luckily my walkway is still mostly shoveled out from when I was home two weeks ago. I walk right through the fresh wall of snow, and it melts into my socks and work shoes. My home is a tiny, hundred-year-old, uninsulated wooden cottage, with a river rock fireplace. It rests by the world's largest seaplane base and is one of only three houses that are directly on the now-frozen lake.

321 seaplanes are in my backyard, and most are currently outfitted with skis. Many are pulled up on shore, unused for the winter with their floats still on. I admire my own Piper Cub waiting faithfully in my yard for our next adventure, and tears of joy overflow, and freeze to my eyelashes. By spring, airplanes will trade their skis for floats. I will splash down in a sapphire lake, hundreds of miles away from anyone. Smelling wild celery root, I'll wade to shore with my fishing pole. The wild, blue geranium and fuchsia fireweed sway in the breeze, while millions of sunlit orbs dance on the frigid water applauding the blooms. It's an explorer's fantasy, hunting for moose horn treasures, fossils, and the elusive oosic. An oosic is the bone of a walrus's penis. They are coveted by bartenders, to install for use as a beer tap.

For now, the pink flamingos at the end of my yard are partially visible, and a section of the lake has been plowed for ice skating. It's ready for my next hot-buttered rum party. I turn the key to my peeling, white-painted wooden door. Inside I'm greeted by the familiar smells of cinnamon potpourri and spent ashes in the fireplace.

I reach for the phone, and my only lead. An alert voice answers "Det Alpha. How can I help?"

"Hi, I'm Ava" I begin "I'm friends with Mio, Wolverine's girlfriend,"

"Mio... right. What does she do again?" The voice is screening me.

"She's a pilot. Like me." I answer. "Look, I know a girl who's in trouble and I heard some of you guys rescue women from human trafficking."

"Usually it's the retired guys that do that." He answers crisply.

"Do you know any of them?" I ask hopefully.

"I can ask around." He offers.

Disappointed, I almost forgot the other reason for my call. I stare at the oversized watch on my bookshelf. "Hey, do you know a guy named Tank?"

"Hey Tank" I hear him yell into the background. "Sure, here ya go."

"Hello?" It's Steve. I can't believe his sexy voice was just a phone call away.

"Hi," I stumble, but recover. "I have your watch."

"Oh hey. I'm glad you called. Where are you?" Steve sounds happy.

"Lake Hood" I reply.

"Oh, you're on a layover." He presumes.

"No, actually I live here," I tell him optimistically.

"Wow, that's great. How'd you know I was here?" Steve asks.

"The inscription on your watch says you're in the Alaska Air Guard." I remind him.

"Actually the watch was a present to me, from the Air Guard here." He continues "They fly me around. Look, I apologize..."

I cut him off. "It's ok. No apology necessary." I feel like I'm being intrusive, "When do you want to pick up your watch?"

"I'm running out the door to surf the bore tide, it starts in an hour," he says cheerfully. "Can I come by and pick it up?"

"Sure." I give him my address and feel the air being sucked out of my lungs. He lives down the street and I'm a wreck. I scan my closet for something sexier than the slacks I wore in business class. I barely spray enough perfume to hide the fact I haven't slept, other than in an airline seat, and he's knocking at my door.

"I'm sorry about the snow." I apologize, realizing he trudged through it to get to my door. "I just walked in from a work trip and didn't get it shoveled out yet."

"Good thing I'm wearing a dry suit" He laughs about his black neoprene ensemble. "I can't believe you live here."

"I can't believe you live here." I raise my eyebrows and hand him his watch.

"Well, I don't live here all the time. My job is crazy." He tries.

"As a piccolo player?" I challenge.

Steve laughs "I can't tell strangers in bars what I do for a living."

I know he's right and silently nod.

He continues to explain, "I'm overseas a lot. In a different country every month"

I shake my head. "I was in ten countries this month." I give him a look, and he knows he can't get off the hook.

"I'm sorry." He's apologetic again, but still so happy-go-lucky. His smile is addictive, and I can't help but melt into his shimmering eyes all over again. "My buddies and I didn't believe you were a pilot. He grimaces. We thought everyone in the red light district bullshits about what they do."

"It's not the first time" I assure him.

"In the morning, I saw your airline uniform and realized you were telling the truth." He looks around at the aviation memorabilia in my home. and admits "I really believe it now. Can we start over? I'm Steve." He says genuinely and extends his competent hand.

"Sure." We shake on it and I add "You were honest with me about your name."

"Sure, just ask my mom." he jokes.

"My buddies are waiting out front." He says, and I try not to feel disappointed. "We gotta run or we'll miss the tidal bore. But if you ever want to go skiing or something?"

"Really? I love skiing." He's inviting, so I'm participating. "I've always wanted to ski Resurrection Pass, but can't find anyone to do it with."

"I've skied it a few times. What are you doing this weekend?" Wow, I love a proactive man.

"I have almost 2 weeks off right now. I'm open" I shrug.

"I'll book the cabins tonight and call you." He starts to bolt.

"Wait. Before you go... I have a friend who needs help. You're in the Special Forces, right? Do you know how to rescue women from human trafficking?"

"I might know a guy" My heart skips at Steve's reply. I forgive him completely now.

"Ok," I smile. "Enjoy your surf. I'll talk to you tonight"

I collapse into my couch, which is a row of seats from a wrecked Russian plane. My eyes trace my familiar treasures in a maze across the room. Photos of my dad flying Navy fighters are framed near his cap and goggles on my mantle. The cap and goggles are saturated with DDT, from crop dusting after the war. He sprayed the dangerous chemical on cotton in Mississippi, with a Stearman. He once told me, there was a leak in the pipe that ran along the cockpit floor. The season was almost over, so he had to fly with the leak spraying DDT in his face for the last couple of hours. The leak was so bad, he had to wipe his goggles to see, every time he crossed a field. He had five hungry, young sons to feed and a wife who stopped caring about anything other than her manicure.

A tailhook lies at the base of my hearth. I received it as a going away present, from a company where I worked as an aircraft mechanic. Beside it rests a piston, that's pitted to death, and caused an engine failure on a DC-3 I was flying. Bookshelves are covered in aircraft technical manuals and warbird magazines. Airplane-shaped Christmas lights sprawl from the curtain rods. I grimace at a photo of Dad's jeep aircraft carrier over the door. It was much too short for the Hellcats he was flying off it. If only Dad could see me now.

I kneel on the floor to build a fire, in my river-rock fireplace. The pine aroma fills my senses, and I acknowledge the chill descending through the soot chimney. The newspaper tinder catches fire, from my could-be-anywhere-hotel bar matches. I wish the sad realities could burn away, as easily as the printed pages.

Steve calls later as promised. "I got the huts reserved. I'm at work but we are getting launched to find some missing ice climbers."

His tone is serious, but mine is urgent. "I know a girl who was kidnapped and sold into sex slavery. I actually saw her the night I met you in Amsterdam, but I didn't know the situation. I need to get her back to her family."

"Is she a runaway?" Steve hurriedly throws out some valid questions. "Is she American?"

"No, and no" I answer.

"I'll call a buddy and see if he can help."

"As a pilot, I can fly free anywhere in the world, that US air carriers go to" I explain "I can jumpseat to Amsterdam and help find her."

"Not a good idea, Ava. Traffickers are bad dudes, and you don't want to risk your own life." I know Steve is right. "We'll have plenty of time to talk on Friday. Let's take two vehicles. We'll leave your truck at the North end of the trail for when we finish. I'll pick you up there, in Hopewood, and drive us the three hours to our starting point, the South end of the trail. Can you be at the Hopewood trailhead at 6 am?"

"Sure" I reply. I love a man with a plan. It's 38 miles one way over the pass, and I wouldn't want to ski that round trip.

Steve sounds reassuring. "See you then."

The International Airport is across the lake. I wake up to the rumble of four engines going into reverse, and

I struggle with fatigue. Need coffee. The time zones have my head turned around, but it's Friday and I want to ski Resurrection Pass. I put it off for a long time because it's not safe to go alone. It's the 16th of March, I have 16 songs on my playlist, and there are 16 guys I really care about. Steve might be number one.

My trusty 1965 Ford pickup cranks right up for the drive to the Hopewood trailhead, and I find Steve already there. I leave my truck parked, so we can drive it out at the end of our trip. It's nice to have a vehicle on both sides. The weather is a crap shoot and we probably won't see another soul.

Once inside Steves's warm truck cab, I admire his brawny build and fleecy hair. Maybe it's just the snuggle weather, but I find myself wanting to rip off all three layers of his clothing. I watch Steve expertly drive the icy, winding, mountain highway, and it feels good to rest. I feel safe with him.

"What's going on with your missing friend, Ava?"

"Well, I don't actually know her," I confess. "I saw her in a window in the Red Light District. Then I had a work trip to Rio for Carnaval and stayed there. The whole country shuts down for a week and just parties, so I decided to also. I started hanging out with some local women, not realizing they were prostitutes."

"We've all been guilty of that" Steve laughs jovially, and only half joking. I feel a pang of jealousy like being socked in the solar plexus with a ball-peen hammer, but my jealousy passes easily. Guys like Steve literally save our country from terrorists every day.

"How do we get her out of Amsterdam?" I question him.

"Do you have a street address?" Steve's the voice of reason.

"I have a map, and can show you the exact block she is on, and I have her photo" I respond.

"Good enough." Steve says "I spoke with my buddy. We were on Green Team together. Now he's out of the Teams and specializes in rescuing people from these situations. He's interested in helping, and he's well-funded. When we get to the trailhead, I'll drop him the coordinates of that block." Steve glances at me with unnecessary concern, "How were your flights?"

"Uneventful. Just like my dad always said they should be." I smile. "I'm very thankful I don't fly around Alaska for work anymore. I don't miss the freezing fog or 70-knot winds. I know you've seen even worse."

"Ya," Steve says nonchalantly. "But there's always somebody next to me, freezing his ass off too. You must've done a lot of bush flying alone?"

"Yes, I feel a stronger bond with certain aircraft than I do with most of my friends." I confess "When you live through near-death experiences with your plane, it becomes your loyal friend."

I continue, "I also flew larger planes that require two pilots, like DC-4s. They were fitted with fuel tanks in the fuselage, for delivering 20,000 lbs of diesel to remote gold mines. I flew with a guy who used to say 'When it's your time to go it's your time to go. But I don't wanna be sitting next to you."' I smile remembering my friend. Rest in peace.

"We carried everything from propane to snowmachines." I reminisced. "The cargo deck was 17 feet above the ground, but some mines didn't have a forklift. So to unload the 115-pound cylinders of propane, my boss would roll them out the door and they'd drop onto a carefully positioned tire. It would bounce and roll and I question my sanity, for being the one on the ground chasing it."

"It's good to be young and dumb", Steve agrees.

"And naive. There was an old miner at Chandler Lake, who had an immense gold nugget he wore around his neck. He said he found the big rock on the way to the outhouse." I feel self-conscious admitting, "I was so naive, I actually believed him."

"Have you been to Squaw Mountain?" Of course, Steve knows all the challenging airstrips.

"Sure, the old military runway with a 200 ft elevation difference between one end and the other." I smile knowingly.

"That's the one" Steve smiles thinking about it also.

"It looks, and feels, like flying into the side of a mountain. The instrument approach plate had "Go-Around Improbable" stamped on it. For landing, you have to flare twice. The take-off felt like the downside of a roller coaster."

"I've only gone in there, in the back of a Blackhawk" Steve humbly admits.

"I miss flying helicopters," I say with jealousy. "I'd kill to fly the ones you've ridden in."

"Sometimes 'riding in them' isn't an accurate term. Stacked like cordwood is more like it." I sense Steve's remembering something he can't talk about. "What's your favorite airstrip in Alaska?"

"Toby Creek mine. It's in a box canyon. There's a C-46 crashed on one side, it caught a wingtip on a hillside. A C-119 crashed on the other side, its nose wheel hit a pothole." I admit "It is a challenge to focus on your touchdown point and ignore the wrecks on both sides of the runway. The surrounding golden hills lull you into feeling it's a beautiful place, but the crooked, gravel runway slips away much too fast. There's not a chance to go around. It's one way in, one way out."

"So it's your favorite because of the adrenaline rush?" Steve asks.

"No." I chuckle "After unloading the fuel, an exceptionally good-looking, young miner would sit down on the runway with me. He'd break out a loaf of bread and a jar of peanut butter, and make me a peanut butter sandwich, he was just so sweet." I finish with a contented sigh

Steve's laughter snaps me out of it. "Wow, is that all it takes to win you over?"

"Ugh, no" I shudder, remembering. "Capital Creek Mine had fantastic food, but a creepy vibe," It was a rutted, half-flooded, excuse of a dirty runway. Steep embankments dislocate your focus and cull you towards a ditch. "It felt like a muddy whirlpool of depression, because of its grimy inhabitants."

"What were they like?" Steve asks curiously.

"It's customary to stay for lunch and exchange news at the mines because they haven't seen another human outside of their camp for weeks." I continue, "These miners ate better than I do at home because they had a proper mess hall and dedicated cooks. We were enjoying meatloaf, mushrooms, and potatoes, with pineapple cheesecake and fresh rhubarb pie. I wanted to compliment the camp cook, so I said 'This is the best pie I've ever had'. That was a mistake." I shake my head wishing I could shake the memory.

"One grubby miner stared hopefully up at me, with his slop-filled spoon poised in mid-air. He hadn't bathed in a week and his matted beard doubled as a napkin. His crooked teeth twitched like a repulsive puzzle." I imitated the miner's southern drawl for Steve to emphasize my point. "We'll cook for ya every night if you'll stay."

Steve teases "You don't want to sleep with filthy workers that haven't seen a woman in months?"

"Nauseated, I realized the other miners were also looking at me as if I were a ham sandwich. All I wanted to do was run, screaming, for the plane."

"That does seem like dangerous bush flying. I'll bet you'd rather get mauled by a bear in Kodiak while offloading spam."

"Yuck, even bears don't eat spam" I exclaim. I had enough bear encounters to know what they eat. Bacon grease is a favorite.

The weather is so bad in places like Kodiak. I flew there for two weeks straight before I ever saw Mt Barometer, the 2500 ft mountain at the end of the sea-level runway. When it's not raining, it's freezing. The ramp is like an ice skating rink, and unloading the freight feels even more dangerous than doing the missed approach. Because of the mountain, the instrument approach has the go-around initiated at two 3.3 miles out. Somehow several aircraft have still managed to hit that mountain. The hundred or so times I flew into Kodiak taught me three things.

1) If your headset quits working, it's because condensation in the microphone froze.
2) If the deicing fluid is dripping all over your boots, you may have to land looking out the side window.
3) If you're T-boned uncontrollably into the wind while taxiing, it's because your wheels are on solid ice & you've been hit by a 70-knot gust.

Driving in Alaska is no picnic either. We weave down the slippery road, and it's disorienting in flat white. It's like driving through a bottle of milk. Occasionally the dark shape of an indifferent mountaintop materializes, and I strain to decipher its steepness. The seriousness of our ski trip sinks in.

"My pack is 40 lbs, how about yours?" I ask.

"A little heavier. I brought a GPS, ice ax, shovel, and rope." Steve explains.

"Rope to tie me up?" I innocently flirt.

"That would be more interesting than ice climbing" Steve looks excited. "I know a lot of intricate knots."

Maybe he likes me too. I have a feeling I'll find out. "The first cabin I booked is about nine miles in. Hopefully, we can be up there with enough daylight to chop wood. The cabins are uninsulated with only wood bunks, wood stoves, and nothing else."

"We stay at the Pass tomorrow night?" I try to clarify, "Over 2000 feet of elevation gain?"

"Yes. I also reserved the Moose cabin after that if we need it, but we probably won't stay there. At that point, we'll be skiing downhill. We could just ski 17 miles in one day rather than stopping."

"Sure, it just depends on the weather." I agree.

We park and hurriedly keep moving to preserve what heat we have. At ten below zero, you can't mess around. Steve's ready first, and calls his friend from the truck cab.

"Thank you so much" I embrace him. His earthy scent is a turn-on, and I appreciate the lack of cologne. This is a real man, not a show-off trying to impress. Steve has nothing to prove and I'm the happiest woman in the world to be here with him. I find a quiet peace in the vastness.

We have climbing skins on our skis because the first nine miles are mostly uphill, in fresh powder and flat white conditions. The overcast means there's no shadow or reference. No one else has been on the trail since the latest snow, so we sink above our knees with every step. It's not skiing at this point, just high-stepping and post-holing through it. It's a two-dimensional world that feels like the bottom is falling out. But carrying our skis would be even worse, because of rocks and uneven terrain beneath. It's a slog.

Flying through whiteout can also be exhausting. It seems as if you're not flying forward, but suspended in place above a frozen ocean, with a frozen windshield.

"At this rate, we're gonna need that third cabin," I suggest between breaths.

"You're doing fine" Steve reassures me. "You've obviously done a lot of this"

"I've done overnight ski trips into the backcountry, alone," I admit. "When I was four years old I had a bucket list. I wanted to climb Mt Everest."

"I haven't climbed Everest," Steve says "But I've climbed Denali a few times. You could handle that no problem. What else was on your childhood bucket list?"

"I wanted to run a marathon and also get a Bachelor's degree," I say sheepishly. "I finally have the money, so I'm finishing my degree right now. I've only run 14 miles at a time, so I'm not sure I'll do a marathon." They seem like such childish dreams to me now. "What about you? Why did you become a SEAL?"

"I'm happiest out in nature, especially mountain climbing. Sleeping in a bivvy sack on the side of a cliff is my favorite place to be." Steve replies. "I also love Scuba and swimming. I get paid to be in challenging areas, with my friends, and heavily armed. It just doesn't get any better. Especially for me. I was a working-class kid, with no college money and no future. I didn't want a mindless, scheduled job. I didn't want to die in the same town I grew up in. I wanted to skydive. As it turns out, I excel at extreme sports."

I'm relieved when we finally see the stovepipe of the Roman cabin sticking up out of the snow. We tunnel down to the door of the buried cabin with Steve's telescoping shovel. Setting up camp, my sweat is starting to freeze. Steve offers to get the fire going, while I gratefully get in my sleeping bag shivering uncontrollably. I'm acclimated to 90 degrees in Rio, so this first night is miserable until my body gets used to subzero. Despite wearing two pairs of long underwear, a wool shirt, and a Gortex winter coat, I curl up into a tight ball. Freezing fingers ooze through the cracks in the cabin, grasping my soul.

Steve melts snow to make cups of instant soup, and it warms me from the inside out. I have to drink it quickly before it freezes. The cabin will take hours to warm up and we'll need to feed it firewood every few hours. This is not even the cold area of AK. Above the Artic Circle, the sun doesn't rise above the horizon during December and January. The average temperature in those months is minus 20 degrees Fahrenheit. In summer it is usually a balmy 50 degrees. Some airports I've frozen at, include Barter Island, Kotzebue, Fort Yukon, and Goodnews Bay. Each one has a smorgasbord of history, peppered with tragic accidents. The translation for Anaktuvuk Pass is literally "The Place of Caribou Droppings".

Since aviation is the lifeline of the backcountry, any village with more than 200 people has a respectable runway of several thousand feet. When the ground thaws in spring, so does the sewage. Bouquets of barrels, tarps, and pallets sprout as reminders. There are only a few months to get work done under the Midnight Sun, and often it snows before projects are finished again. By September, the sunlight barely oozes out, like a thick, foreboding honey. Much of the state looks like a bowl of Fruit Loops, in scarlet, purple, and gold before decaying under the snowy pall of winter's casket. I carry that casket off to sleep with me.

Sun's fingers brush the snow
Gently off her mountain hair.
My skis are only witness
To the resurrection there.
On a Corcovado sunrise
Lenticulars hug the pass.
They blow their wings out laughing
At my follied trail-break dash.
Sundogs of mauve and green,
Chasing their own tails,
Bark down the white rabbit
Who kindly broke my trails.
Wrought with iron flowers
Wrung from subzeros night
Steely bells from frozen hells
Are peeling out of sight.
They're laughing with my child-like joy.
Laughing as I fall
Through geometric pine trees
Wonderland's checkered hall.
I laugh back

For I'm not cold,
And no mountain is too high.
My skis have wings and my voice sings
With the wind, the stars, the sky.
Towards distant glowing mountains
Under oceans running deep,
I slide down her snowy, sun-laced face
To the life I choose to keep.

Chapter 5

Every alarm on the 747's flight deck is ringing and only compounds my joy. The Ground Proximity Warning System is commanding "Whoop, whoop, pull-up". The Collision Avoidance System alerts "traffic, traffic, climb, climb now". Red and amber lights flash all over the console and I rock my airplane's wings for all it's worth. My adrenaline is exuberantly wired in with the sirens. The bells and whistles only heighten the moment, because I'm buzzing a US aircraft carrier, legally.

It started on a layover in Hong Kong. I was enjoying a meal at my favorite Italian restaurant. My dinner companion was an oil painting of a Mediterranean woman, with a mustache. The lamb Osso Buco was melting in my mouth, when I noticed a tasty-looking fellow walk by. This was not normal. I notice some more good-looking men roaming around outside. At first, it was only a couple of glimpses, but they started oozing in like spaghetti through a colander.

I thought I ordered the "hot tea", but I was really getting the hotties. They gush around the red and white checkerboard tables. I've been to Hong Kong hundreds of times but have never seen such biologically appropriate specimens. The British have been scarce since the reclamation, but these guys aren't British. None of them are wearing skinny jeans.

It occurs to me that statistically, I should be able to target a potential boyfriend tonight. My relationship with Steve didn't progress during our ski trip. A freak warm front came through and it rained on the third day. We ended up walking downhill in our ski boots on solid ice, carrying our skies. The last few miles were in darkness, but we were just trying to get out before our wet clothes froze again.

Some provocative guys take a seat adjacent to me. They possess the overconfident personage, bred into military pilots since the beginning of their flight training. But I suspect they're born with it. I try not to stare, but curiosity always kills me. I finish my meal and slide up to their table. At first, the guys are suspicious. The US military is brainwashed to be wary of friendly strangers overseas, and with good reason. I suspect I'm right about them, since they introduce themselves as Anteater, Belly Flop, Ahab, and Blower. I am overjoyed when Belly Flop pulls out a challenge coin. Of course, they're pilots.

Luckily I keep a challenge coin in my purse for emergencies like this. When a coin is presented, everyone else must show theirs too, or else buy a round of drinks. Unfortunately for Belly Flop, since we all have coins on us, his challenge backfired and now he has to buy the round.

"Are you a pilot?" Ahab looks at me as if he's never seen a chic pilot before.

"I am" I smile "but I fly a 747, not a Stealth."

The guys examine my B-2 coin that reads "When it absolutely, positively has to be taken out overnight."

"Cool," Ahab is curious "Who gave you this?"

"One of the Stealth pilots I dated." I admit carefully "It was the guy who had to eject over the Tampa Bay airshow. Do you remember? his aileron failed."

"I remember that" answers Blower "All the Stealths were grounded for a while for inspection. Cracks were found in several other ailerons."

"Exactly" I confirm. "The first thing he said when he parachuted to the ground was 'Is anyone hurt?' because that's the kind of guy he was. He was so nice. He only cared if people were safe from his broken jet when it crashed."

Belly Flop returns with a round of drinks, and I fail at suggesting an appropriate toast. "What is it you guys say? No one ever drowned in their own sweat?"

They grimace, and Belly Flop answers with "Fight through mud, fuck through blood." Good American Marines, always up for a drink and a laugh. They've adopted me into their group now. After all, they've been on a carrier for months. Most of the other sailors are already lodged in the cat-houses of the slanted snatch. These boys are either good, or fast.

Their acceptance of me is the best feeling in the world. Often I don't receive it from my own crew, because some men think women don't belong in the cockpit, even though it was named after us.

Often, men don't discriminate on purpose, they're just looking for the perfect Minnie-Me upon which to impart their grandiose wisdom, and I'm not a Dick. I had one simulator instructor who was super nice to me, but he never looked at me during the pilot briefing. He would only look at my sim partner while he briefed us. I didn't really care, but my sim partner noticed and he wanted to try an experiment. For the next briefing, my sim partner would turn his head and stare at me. It actually worked. the instructor would finally, unconsciously, turn and look at me while he was instructing.

More flyboys strut over to join us. It turns out that some fly Harriers, but some fly Cobra helicopters. "Helicopter flying is my true love," I exclaim.

"You fly them too?" Blower asks. I'm fantasizing about how good he must look wearing his flight suit. There's a reason they call it a three-foot zipper and he is built like a Viking. Blond, tan, and I'd love to bounce a quarter off his ass.

I tell Blower about my dreams. "For most of my life, I never even considered helicopters. Then, when I was 23 years old, I had three helicopter dreams in one month. In each dream, flying them felt so much more intuitive than fixed-wing. Unfortunately, I spent all my time and money getting fixed-wing licenses. I was too broke to switch to helicopters. But now I have my commercial rotorcraft license" I add smiling.

Blower's milk chocolate eyes are riveting. I slide into them, trying to decide if there's room for me inside his life. His mannerisms are rugged yet precise, without being forceful. I check his empty ring finger and scan a few other places too. I imagine his jawline in my fingers. What would it be like to taste his kisses? His blond hair is short and spiky, like days that are too much fun. Days like this one.

"My girlfriend back home has a private pilot's license." Blower tells me, snapping me out of it. "She said that during her flight training, someone responded to her voice on the radio by transmitting in the blind 'Another empty kitchen.' Do you hear stuff like that flying commercially?"

"The first time I went into Cairo, their approach control wouldn't even speak to me," I tell him. "After the third failed attempt to raise them on the radio, my captain said 'I'll take the radios, it's your landing now.' Of course, they answered him right away. I was hand-flying then, and it turned out to be super fun because the Egyptians vectored us around, as "punishment" for my gender. So I got a grand tour of the pyramids and saw things I didn't even know existed."

I continue "But as far as my coworkers, there's always a percentage." I give an example. "I met one guy who said 'We already have two women pilots here. One's a bitch and can't fly for shit, and the other just can't fly for shit." But I was glad he said that, because then I knew I couldn't trust him. It's the ones who pretend to be your friend that you have to worry about.

"I love that you're not jaded by it. You're definitely a glass-half-full person. What are you doing tomorrow?" Blower's questions.

"I'm flying to Dubai tomorrow at noon, and then on to Sydney." I hate to even say it. I want to stay in

Hong Kong with them, and experience the camaraderie they share.

"Sydney" Belly Flop steps in. "That sounds like an awesome gig. Maybe when I retire from this, I'll fly freight instead of passengers. If you don't mind me asking, what are the requirements?"

"The requirements are the same as an airline job, but The quality of life is better. I can live wherever I want, rather than having to live near a base city, or commute." I explain. "The company buys tickets from my home to wherever my trip starts, and ends. Cargo is also better because the boxes don't bitch."

The guys nod in agreement. They don't relish the thought of crazy passengers causing inflight emergencies. But getting crazy on the ground is different. Anteater exclaims "The World Cup is starting soon. We need to go to the pub."

"Everyone's next door, at O'Hare's." Ahab tells me. We settle up our tabs to leave.

"So Ahab, how'd you get your call sign?" I naively ask. Their giggles follow Ahab's expression, as he wonders how to break it to me.

"He likes the larger women," Anteater says with plenty of hand gestures and spelling out the acronym for me, "Another Huge Ass Bitch."

"Why are you an Anteater?" I ask, trying to move on.

Ahab gets payback on him, "Let's just say he's not Jewish."

I blush and decide to stop asking about their callsigns. Entering O'Hare's pub, about twenty helicopter pilots have set up shop in the back room, surrounded by big-screen TVs and Guinness signs. Then my education really begins.

Inspired by the Irish team playing in the World Cup soccer, Blower feels his Irish is up. He takes off his leather boot and holds it up with a proclamation. "Time to shoot the boot" he bellows.

Sounding like red-blooded cheerleaders, the pilots applaud and pour their varied beers into his shoe. The forthcoming cadence shudders my soul, like a stick shaker during the stall, "Shoot the boot", they demand over and over again in unison. Blower guzzles the musky mixture without taking a breath. To my squeamish horror, his smelly footwear is passed on to the next guy, and I'm sitting next to him.

Like bloodthirsty lions at the Coliseum, the relentless mob refills the brewing sole. I observe with technical trepidation. It's obvious I'll have to repeat the maneuver momentarily, and it's all happening so fast. My turn. I inhale my last few breaths and focus on patriotism. Voluminous cheers fill the air as the fighting men struggle to pour their malted concoctions into Blower's shoe, which I now hold in my hands.

The sour leathery mash is not as rancid as I expected. I gulp the barley brew from the bottomless boot. Eventually, I am forced to breathe through my nose. My eyes tear with sudsy fermentation. I dare not choke, the guys are watching me. Dozens of fingers rhythmically wag in unison to the bawl, "Shoot the boot, Shoot the boot, Shoot the boot". It roars in my ears and brings courage. The smell is reminiscent of my childhood when my brothers would pin me down while scrunching their well-worn socks up my nostrils.

The brew decays down my throat, and I try not to think about the bacteria. Hopefully, the elixir is distilling the ills. At last, the chowdered chalice is bereft. I wipe my lips to the triumphant howls, and pass the boot. Checking my watch, it's almost 10 pm. I have to be in the limo to the airport in 12 hours. I wish I didn't have to leave.

I opt for an Irish goodbye and duck out of the noisy pub. The sewer smells of Hong Kong blast me in the face. It smells like rotten seafood, feces, and fried lizard on a stick. I try to call Steve. No answer.

I stare out my Kowloon hotel room with its spectacular view of Hong Kong island. The lights are hypnotizing and unlike me, they never get old. My phone rings but I don't recognize the number. "Sorry Ava, I can't talk on that phone," It's Steve.

"Ok. Did your friend find Monique?" I ask.

"Monique was moved. She's no longer in Amsterdam." He's dead serious.

"What?" I choke in disbelief. "I thought this was a done deal."

"My buddy and his team are familiar with Amsterdam. They found out who her owner was, where he came from, and who his friends are. He's part of a larger organization, and they move their girls a lot." Steve continues, "Monique was gone, so they grabbed his number one girl. She talked in exchange for freedom.

The girl claimed Monique was sold to a group of sheiks in Dubai."

I'm going to Dubai tomorrow." I exclaim.

"Don't even think about it." Steve is alarmed. "I'll help my buddy find her. This is way over your head. You could be killed, or worse."

"I'll be there anyway." I insist, "I'm always with my crew, and they are hooker magnets. I go to Dubai a lot, and it's safer than New York City because of all their strict rules."

"Ava." Steve pauses. "How would you get her out of the United Arab Emirates?" He emphasizes the word Arab.

"I have loadmasters and mechanics that smuggle Jaguar furs and Turkish shotguns in tool compartments. I can get her out." I am just as adamant.

"Think through this, Ava. How is she gonna get past security at the airport, so you can hide her on your plane?" Steve has a point.

Ideas start to flow. "I see many women here wearing those full-length Thabs. I could cover her up with a Thab, but she probably doesn't have a passport." I realize.

"Exactly. The guys who bought her probably have a forged passport. But she doesn't have that. You can't take her to your hotel, or anywhere. They'll follow you, and you're on camera wherever you go." Steve is the voice of reason.

"I was looking on the internet," I suggest. "There are non-profit groups that care about this, maybe we should involve them?"

"Those groups fund my friend and others like him. They can't get her out of the Emirates any more than he can." Steve reasons. "Almost a million people are sold into sex slavery each year. Half of them are children. Monique is not a citizen of a first-world country, and right now, you are the only person advocating for her."

Hanging up with Steve I feel distraught and helpless. I need to do something. I need to calibrate myself. Am I normally a helpless person or a strong person? Strong. Am I normally lacking, or resourceful? Resourceful. It can't be coincidental that I'm flying to Dubai tomorrow. It must be my destiny to rescue Monique. If I find her, I will get her out myself.

During my pre-flight briefing, I warn my crew that military friends are anchored up somewhere in the huge, horrible harbor. I feel we must give them a proper send-off. I'm mentally prepared to rock our wings in salutation if we happen to spot the mighty ship. I know Captain Lark approves. I've flown with him a ton and he's always up for some fun. My ex-Air Force flight engineer, Dyers, says it will never happen. Who would be mindless enough to steer a US aircraft carrier, under the departure flight route of Hong Kong's International Airport?

Lifting my giant aircraft off the asphalt-covered landfill, optimism fades to the gray skies above. Forgetting my wishful thinking, I hunker down to the task at hand, guiding my behemoth aircraft through the invisible airways of the departure profile. No sooner have we cast off the sewer smells below, when Dyers announces my new friends are actually right off our bow, on runway heading. He's half standing up, scanning the harbor. Because of the steep angle of attack used for take-off, I can't see them.

I'm hand-flying and buckled in my five-point harness, so I stay seated. "Tell me when we're almost over them," I say excitedly.

"Now" Dyers announces.

I frugally gather a few extra knots of airspeed by settling the nose down a few degrees, then thrust the ailerons from side to side. I'm rewarded when all hell breaks loose with our radar and warning systems, which unequivocally means we are directly above the floating metropolis. I hope our brothers in arms appreciate the 231-foot-long wave, at less than a thousand feet. I'm betting they noticed, especially if their radar was going haywire with warning sirens as well. I feel like Cinderella flying a big, doomed pumpkin, and wish I had a glass slipper to drop.

Once airborne to Dubai, I feel hopeful. Captain Lark always tells jokes in flight. Most of them are running commentaries. It makes the nine hours of boredom fly by. For this leg, his task is mostly navigation and radios. Which seriously just consists of repeating frequencies all day. Each time we cross into a new region of airspace, the controller hands us off to the next one. At the boundary, we hear, "Solar 412, contact Mumbai Control on 120.65"

"120.65, Solar 412." Lark answers, then unclicks the mic, "Oh look it's the aurora borealis. As a whore you bore me Alice. Get it? Get it?"

Click. Lark says politely "Mumbai Control, Solar 412, Flight Level 350" Unclick. "Daddy, can we fuck the puppies? Go ask your mother."

It's better than a nine-to-five office job. We are chasing time zones backward, as we fly to the West. I embrace the solitude and accept the handfuls of turbulence glancing off towering cumulus. I wish I could stay up here forever. No bills to pay or lonely bed to collapse into. No feeling of defeat, surrendering to an empty apartment with an empty refrigerator. No vicious gravity or obstacles to tiptoe around. Only joy, skimming the atmosphere's rouge, pigmented landscape.

The promenade of airplanes, parades between cities with great self-importance. We crossed imaginary waypoints and roundabout holding patterns. Passing middle-marker signposts we descend out of the highway in the sky, to the local streets of final approach. There are stormy tunnels, streetlamps of sunlight, and bridges of blue sky.

The Persian Gulf's turbulence rocks our 547,300lb cradle. We've burned about 26,500 pounds of fuel per hour. The endless expanse of sand squats flatly below us, lifeless. A black hole of night. I don't understand how people can make a living in the desert. Lacking reference points, the infinite wasteland seems to swallow us whole as we descend into its doughy, warm bowels.

Lark stops telling jokes for three seconds. "Dubai Tower, Solar 412, ILS 22 Left."

"Solar 412, Dubai Tower, 22 Left, clear to land, wind 290 at 15" is the welcome reply.

"Gear down, flaps 25, landing checklist" I command in between laughing at Lark's jokes.

"Gear down, in, green light, speed brake armed, flaps 25, green light."

Dyers adds his confirmation, "Engine ignition, flight start. Hydraulic pressure and quantity, are normal. Landing checklist complete."

The automated, deep voice of the ship's computer, confirms my height above the ground, "1000".

As we settle into a pillow of ground effect, the ship continues its automated announcements of our radar altimeter. "50, 40, 30, 20... 10" If I flare just right, there's a pause right before the ten-foot alert. We touch down like a butterfly with sore feet and I pull the reversers back.

I sigh upon landing, feeling betrayed by the earth's hold on me. I'm probably more understood by air traffic controllers, than by my own neighbors. I remove my headset feeling melancholy as their last words fade.

When we get our room keys, Lark announces "We're going to the Hurricane Club. Lobby in 30."

The line for the club grows longer by the minute. Halfway to the entrance, I realize there's another line besides ours, and it's only women. I peer through the darkness at the line I'm in. It's all men, other than me.

I alert my crew "There's a women's line and a men's line. I'm in the wrong line."

Lark responds "Just stay with us".

"Right" I agree, "Why would I go stand next to women I don't even know? Plus we're going dancing. Isn't that illegal here? I don't understand this place."

A big surprise waits at the door. One of the bouncers says "You can't come in. You're wearing a skirt"

"Skirts are forbidden inside this bar?" I say in disbelief. "I saw women wearing skirts at my hotel." My voice trails off and I look apologetically at my crew, who hadn't noticed. We look over at the line of women and they're all wearing pants.

"Wait a moment," he says.

I realize my mistake. Walking around in public, I always wear long pants and keep my shoulders covered. I respect the traditions of places I layover, such as the United Arab Emirates, Bahrain, and Kuwait. But we took a taxi to this nightclub, and I thought it was normal to wear a dress out dancing. My eyes dart around for hidden cameras or an all-seeing magistrate who is observing me. I was trying to stay under the radar and find Monique, but now I'm attracting unwanted attention.

I feel like an idiot, and tell my crew "It's ok you guys, I'll just get a taxi back to the hotel"

The bouncer reappears. "It's ok. You can go inside."

My confusion falls by the wayside, as I fetch a round of drinks. I need to decompress. Naivety shields me like a force field. The swirling colored lights of the dance floor hypnotize me, reducing me to an aboriginal primate. According to my own traditions, life is too short to wear a long skirt.

It isn't overly crowded. Enough dancers to free the self-conscious, and not too many to threaten unconsciousness. The nebulous club is highlighted with fluorescent, cerulean water tubes full of bubbles in motion. Dancing with Lark protects me from the unwanted, and makes me desirous to the wanted. I go for another round and carry one to Dyers, who's perched at a ringside table. Four or five women are gathered around him. To my wonderment, they scatter like cockroaches when I approach. I don't stay and chat. The music is too loud.

In the tiled restroom, the bass of the music vibrates the walls. There's a long line for the bathroom stalls. I am intrigued by the ethnic diversity. I strain to recognize the echoed voices. I hear Russian, Latin, and Asian dialects. I marvel at the unity of worldwide women, I ponder the potential for epic, creative brainstorming. What an ideal situation to solve all of the world's problems through international collaboration.

Abruptly, the room tips in my mind and the music's vibrating molecules swell and shift. The mirrors of primping women seem warped, like in a carnival funhouse. The figures morph into their authentic form. My rosy-colored, juvenile glasses shatter to the floor. I foolishly grope at the truth- it's like a Miss Universe Hooker Pageant in here. This isn't a nightclub, it's an entire whorehouse. Someone here must have seen Monique.

I pull her crumpled photo from my satchel. I am behind two women speaking Russian. I surmise they know English. After all, I live in Alaska so we're practically neighbors. I decide a Kiwi phrase is safer. Everyone loves the friendly and harmless New Zealanders. "Hello, How ya going?" I smile. They ignore me.

I try again "You are beautiful women. Beautiful women should wear beautiful dresses." They look at me like I'm crazy.

I turn to the woman who's behind me in line. "Excuse me. Have you seen my friend?" I show her the photo. She looks confused as if she wonders why I'm speaking to her. Other women are staring at me and decide to shut up. What if I'm endangering them? They have no idea who they can trust. Steve was right, this is dangerous for me.

These women may have been offered jobs as a Hostess, on an Entertainer Visa. They didn't realize their new boss was actually their new owner, until he took their passport, locked them up, and pocketed their hard-earned cash. But these girls must be organized by pimps who pay them well. They don't look like scared victims, they seem relatively happy. It's the world's oldest institution because no one can change it, especially not me.

Sometimes walking around Middle Eastern countries, I see women with chains around their waists, underneath their Thabs. How ironic a culture that perpetrates female genital mutilation, legalizes prostitution in sanctioned nightclubs. I wish for a way to educate, and economically liberate the women who aren't allowed to read, write, or drive a car. Is their choice to live with it, or die? Who has more freedom, the local Muslim women covered in robes and chains, or these working girls?

Back on the dancefloor, a strapping British guy stumbles upon me. His cross-eyes sway with his beer-saturated body, as he leans his drunken weight on me. "I'm not a hooker", I shout against the music. He doesn't seem to understand my American accent. I try again. By the third try, I'm laughing. I like him, but I want to make it clear I'm not for rent.

He isn't laughing, he's angry. "Then you're the only woman in here who isn't."

I easily escape from him. Unfortunately, the next-suited suitor is downright scary. Sleaze oozes from the lapels of the swine. He reeks of cheap cologne and his short mustache can't hide his hummus breath, "I noticed you're not one of the regular girls".

Nausea reverberates up my spine. I want to run, but feign indifference. "No hablo Ingles," I frown and push my way past him like a runway model.

Approaching Dyers, his harem gallops away in their heels. I'm now offended they're running from me, but losing patience is a virtue at 4 AM. "Why do the hookers flee every time I come to talk to you?"

"I told them you're my daughter", Dyers drawls. "I like flirting with them, but I don't want to sleep with them. I'm happy when you come back."

"Well, I'm outta here. Some slimy guy, who probably already has five wives, just hit on me. See you tomorrow."

"Wait, I'm coming with you." He says and I breathe a sigh of relief. Hailing a cab alone, outside a foreign prostitution club during the witching hour, isn't on my list of safe activities. Lark wants to go too. I appreciate these guys don't cheat on their wives.

Sometime after the Muslim's first call to prayer, Screw Scheduling calls me. "We need to commercial you to Honolulu right now. You will operate a flight to Osan after your legal rest" the familiar voice says.

"Wow, must be important" I wonder "Who called in sick?"

"I can't say" my scheduler sounds uncomfortable. "You're hauling Patriot missiles with Bohan and Macritt. Your limo to the airport is in two hours."

At least I have time for breakfast. I enter the hotel restaurant scanning for co-workers. The decor is mostly charcoal-colored glass with beige leather seats. Lamps of mock basketry, encroach on marbled floors. Lark is there. Or maybe he's still there. I only left him a few hours ago from a nightcap, sitting in the same booth.

"I'm getting commercialed to Hawaii, someone called in sick on a DoD contract," I inform him.

"Good, hopefully I'll get an extra day or two here until they replace you. Wait a minute, Hawaii?" Lark doesn't even try to control his bubbling laughter. Laughter and loud conversation are forbidden in Muslim countries so I glance around uneasily. "Didn't you hear? Toncin overdosed on Viagra last night in Honolulu. They took him off the plane in an ambulance. That's who you're replacing."

My mouth is agape, and Lark is still cracking up. "His crew said he was dizzy and had chest pain so they called 911. By the time the medics carried him away, he confessed to taking too many of the blue diamonds."

"That doesn't surprise me" I shake my head and lower my voice. "That guy is such a predator. He did an unwanted strip tease for me, on the upper deck. We were operating with an extra crew and were on break. I went down to the main cargo deck to get away from him but he followed me. He's a great-looking guy, but he's married. I wouldn't even consider what he wanted. Within five minutes he had his cock out, stroking it, and gizzed all over a pallet of freight."

"Oh, that poor loadmaster" Lark exclaims, "and poor you"

"It's ok" I smirk "It inspired me to poetry..."

Flight of a feather

Airborne in 2.1

Banked like a river

Feet to the horizon

Whistling turbine, tickling my spine

Red desert sunset, sands design

Divine.

The endless, oneness, love that I find

Torching the sky

Smooth and sublime

Somewhere in a jet-drunk, rocketing mind

I am cuming all over myself and mankind

Chapter 6

Waikiki's coral-blanched sand feels gritty between my toes. I stride wistfully along the shore, where foaming edges of the ocean, gurgle and retreat. Moist, citrusy air is palpable on my tongue, and a sensual breeze embraces my sun-splattered skin. My hair is salted and curled from body surfing. A plumeria flower dangles haphazardly from it. I love getting paid to be here, although it can be the loneliest layover on earth. It's ironic seeing all the delusional honeymooners clinking cocktails and believing that another person can make them happy. I don't depend on anyone except myself for happiness. If I found someone to have a relationship with, it would enhance my life, but I wouldn't hold them responsible for how it goes.

Often in a tropical paradise, there aren't any single men in sight, but not today. Today I forget about my usual intentions of bouncing in a catamaran's netting with bottomless mai tais because a steady stream of young minnows is trickling down the beach walk between palm trees. I notice a tempting morsel swim by, followed by even better-looking aquamen. They might as well carry Neptune's trident, as they blatantly scope out my red bikini & sarong.

Suddenly they're gushing around me. They circle, and school up. A well-built sailor approaches me. "I've been on an aircraft carrier for six months. Do you have a hotel room? Take me there and I promise you'll have multiple orgasms."

My body says "Hoo-ya". My mind says- do you really want a minnow? The long pause is embarrassing for us both. Stammering, I walk on, "Thanks anyway, bye."

I want the sharks. My blood simmers now with a tickling sensation. The thrill of hunting an elusive specimen of men suddenly thrills me. The Marine pilots in Hong Kong were just practice. I watch over my shoulder as Minnow is now pleading with another woman. He closes the deal. His friends and some on-lookers cheer as the happy couple rush off together.

My prey would choose the more popular end of the strand. They're bound to be treading water between here and the Shoeless Bar. Almost there, I smell the unmistakable testosterone of night carrier landings. Suntan oil is mixed with the musky sweat of a thousand catapult shots. Leaning against a ledge, right in front of my favorite restaurant, the Sandpiper, my sharks are circling.

Three shirtless, athletic, sex bombs at my two o'clock position. I redirect my flight path for interception. They are tanned, colossal, and unsuspecting at twenty yards and closing. My radar tunes into their conversation.

The pilots are shooting off their wristwatches, discussing tactics, and retelling stories. I'm on final approach and break a sweat. Whisking off my sarong, I reveal my irresistible tattoo of a WW2 Navy fighter. Guns armed.

Stopping and looking both ways down the beach, I pretend to take a photo of Diamondhead. Prepare to fire. They cock their heads, stare at my ink, and the mustached one says "F–8 Bearcat".

His tall, bald friend with translucent blue eyes challenges "Maybe, or it could be a P–47".

I pivot towards the first guy. "You're right, it's a Bearcat. Not many people know that." Attempting to hide my joy, is like them trying to keep their embossed manhood under wraps in their board shorts.

The winner extends a handshake, "My friends call me Sharky. You look like you need a cold beer." His voice is husky, matching his physique.

"You're right. But unfortunately, I have to fly tomorrow." I extract pity slowly, through a syringe of curiosity. "My countdown from bottle to throttle starts at eight."

"Oh, you're a pilot too, Where are you headed?" He's on the hook and I reel him in.

"Ruksan Air Base, I haul rubber dog shit in a 747. It's civilian contract." Acknowledging my inferiority as a freight dog, allows their egos to remain unscathed. "What about you guys?"

"Our carrier is parked near Pole's Point." He tells me. His eyes are milky blue, like a glacier. His dark hair is silver in a few spots, so I'd guess he is a higher rank than the others.

I name-drop to get the conversation going. "You guys might know a friend of mine, Roger Ball."

Sharky's unable to contain his brotherly affection. "He's our ex-Wing Commander. How do you know him?"

"I did aerial firefighting near his ranch in Washington. We did aerobatics in his open-cockpit biplane sometimes, it was an Acrosport. I know his wife and son, too." I add, so they know I'm not a mistress, but Roger wouldn't cheat on his wife for all the hookers in Rio.

I order a Hawaiian Island Iced Tea, and Sharky retains my interest with his enticing charisma. He bites down suggestively on my cherry, and pulls it into his mouth with the stem on. Sharky gazes at me, while I watch him maneuver his tongue. Pulling just the stem out of his mouth, he proudly displays it. He tied the stem into a knot with his tongue and I'm in love.

Somehow the F-18 pilots seem even more masculine, by wearing traditional garlands of orchid flowers. Sharky adorns me with one. He must understand my need to get leid. It turns out that Sharky is the Squadron Commander, and I'm getting turned on just standing next to him. Here I am, having a full-fledged, lifetime fantasy come true. Tiki torches are lit, and a pineapple sunset splashes into the Mai Tai ocean. Birds of paradise and ginger flowers, sprout from every corner. Ukulele music trickles by, and enchanted voices mingle with the surf. We watch for the mirage of the green flash together, and are rewarded by its blaze. About a dozen of us gather at the seaside tables of the restaurant. We feast on ribeyes and moonfish from the open grills, where we season and cook the meat ourselves- the Sandpiper's claim to fame.

Diamond Head's silhouette fades above the shimmering sea of hotel lights. Sharky becomes more affectionate as the night, and the drinks, wear on. At dusk, fireworks besiege us with booming colors that stain the sky and dribble hot tracers upon our upturned faces. I was having such an unforgettable time, I forgot it was Friday. Their drunken disclosures are illuminated with the fizzling fireworks. Exposed, like a field of floodlit dandelions gone to seed, being tilled by a plow of revolving explosions, cultivating our minds.

"Shore leave ends in two hours. Who's gonna sober up and drive?" Asks a voice of reason.

"I'm practically sober," I remind them. "I've been drinking water for the last two hours."

"We borrowed a van and need to return it on base" Sharky explains. "We'll pay for your taxi back to Waikiki, if you drive us to where the van needs to be parked" He offers.

"That's not necessary. You guys pay with your lives by being stuck out at sea for six months straight. It's the least I can do." Their murmurs of appreciation are enough.

"How do you get on and off base, after you fly in?" Sharky's immersed in thought.

"I have a DOD card" I reply, pulling my Department of Defense identity card out of my satchel.

"Shit. She's a Major," he announces, examining it.

"I am?" I honestly didn't realize what the numbers on my ID meant.

"It says so right here. You're an O4." He shows me.

"Oh, I never knew what that was" I explain. "We fly into US air bases, but we aren't allowed to stay in barracks housing. Our company always buys us hotel rooms off base. That's why they issue us DOD cards, so we can get on and off base."

"You mentioned flying to places like Saudi, and Oman. You stay off base there?" He wonders.

"No, those places must be dangerous because when we fly there, we drop our freight and fly the plane empty to somewhere safer, like Kuwait."

"You outrank most of us." someone says, and the silence agrees with him. Ouch. I don't mean to. I'm more comfortable letting these guys feel superior. After all, I didn't even have to go through boot camp.

I try to play it down. "Well, everything's relative. It's not like I'm flying into Afghanistan getting shot at, like you guys."

"I've been curious since 9-11, about the safety of our ship." Sharky ponders. "I really wonder how secure it is. How hard would it be for a terrorist to sneak onboard in port?" the others nod in agreement.

All I'm curious about is how safe I'd feel curled up on his broad chest with those strong arms around me. I crave intimacy. I remember seeing a couple, riding next to each other on their motorcycles. It was a dark, empty street, and no one else was around. They came to a red light and reached out, holding each other's hand until the light turned green. That's the kind of romance I want.

I smile at Sharky, and the thrill is mirrored in his eyes. "I'd like to see if you can walk on board our ship with us. As a test of our ship's security." He announces.

I would follow him anywhere, but before I realize the severity of the situation, Sharky tosses me his golf clubs. Someone else produces dirty laundry for me to carry, and I have childhood flashbacks all over again. Stepping up to the guard shack, I fear I've overdosed on passion fruit juice and pheromones. The security guards inspect each of our ID cards for about three seconds as we file past, and onboard we go.

I'm not even noticed. Embedded within Sharky's pack, I'm smuggled onto a Nimitz class supercarrier, disguised as a drunken sailor. I scuttle up and down gray ladders with my fighter pilot escorts, clutching clubs and duffels. Feeling like a mouse in a maze, I fear becoming lost in the underwater labyrinth of sardine chambers. Most of the guys head to their rooms, but Sharky knows what I want. We think so much alike.

The inky, water-cooled, flight deck is a welcome relief. The breeze is blowing from a hollow emptiness. Or am I experiencing the collective loneliness of a thousand seamen returning to their floating prison? The sight of the Hornets calms me instantly, and I know it's worth the risk to be here.

Careful not to trip over the various hazards on deck, Sharky guides me straight to #30, the F-18 decorated with a flaming American flag on its nose. "This is the first aircraft to bomb Afghanistan after Sept 11," Sharky whispers solemnly. Listening to the wind and silence, I'm awed beyond words. I stroke the fuselage, appreciating every detail and hour of labor, that went into crafting this stoic fighter. I think of my Dad and wish he could see how far Naval technology has come.

It's surprising there's hardly anyone else on the starlit flightdeck. I guess if it's your rooftop, you just enjoy the silence when the million-dollar catapult isn't launching flights. After a few photo ops with #30, Sharky and I stroll hand in hand, as if longtime lovers on a familiar walk. We walk slowly, admiring the swarm of Hornets, and sub-hunting Prowlers, to the E-2 with the sugar cookie radar disc on top. I'm so enthralled and appreciative for this moment, it's difficult to leave and go below deck.

Sharky shows me to his quarters. It's appalling how tiny the officer's rooms are. It makes my bathroom at home look like a penthouse suite. The enlisted men and women must be suffering in their bunks. Before I can fathom what onboard life must be like, Sharky's behind me nipping my neck with soft kisses. Electrifying shivers flex my spine. He holds me the way all women want to be held. My eyes fall on his nightstand, and I see a family photo. Sharky fumbles with the strings to my bikini, and my heart, but I'm straining to see his photo. He looks really happy with a couple of smiling kids and a blonde who must be his wife. Dogfish. I claustrophobically rethink how to escape this situation.

"I've got half an hour to find my way off this ship, or I'll be locked in" I gasp, allowing the cold metal of the bunk rails to enter through my hands, and cool my jets. He wants a quickie, and is probably married. I test the probability of a future with him, "I'm going into days off after this flight. I could meet up with you when you're Stateside next week."

Sharky takes me by the hand and leads me out. Every person in passing seems like a potential whistle-blower, and the risk is staggering. I appreciate the hospitality, but technically I'm a stowaway on a classified, armored, and mobile US Navy air base. Besides, I have to fly in the morning.

Outside my taxi's window, the ladies of the night sachet along Waikiki's strip, with empty hands but full pockets. I can still feel Sharky. I can taste him, and hear his voice as I arrive at my lonely hotel room. I slide my room key down the electronic slot. Buzz, click.

I'm stunned there are people in my room, and one of them is a cop. I'm frozen. Is this really my room? Did the military police know I was on the ship? Will I go to the brig, instead of to jail?

A suited man asks, "Is this your room?"

"Yes." I must look as though they've already hit me with a stun gun.

He turns to face me, becoming gentler. "I'm the hotel manager. The DEA led a drug bust on the room next door to yours."

A Hawaiian officer takes over, "After the raid, I was on the balcony in the next room, looking into adjoining rooms like yours, to see if anyone escaped by hopping over the rail. The lights were on in your room, and it looked like this."

"Is this how you left your room, Ma'am?" Asks the hotel manager.

I'm laughing hard enough to shake all 26 floors of the Sheriott Hotel Waikiki. "What are you guys? The clean police? Yes, this is how I left my room."

I decompress with relief and continue my happy rant. "I'm much too busy, to waste any time picking up my things or organizing my luggage." The authorities shake their heads and apologize for the inconvenience on their way out. Thank goodness they thought my room had been ransacked. If only they knew what I'd really been doing.

Shades of turquoise melding your wake
Faced into wind, freedom at stake
Shoulders set with heavy load
Thousands of soldiers in silent code
Blue diamond's underway, with dawn you are free
No scud to grieve you, destination the sea
Float upon waves, breeze through your hair
Leis left behind with landlocked cares
Prowlers protecting from enemy harms
Hornet's scream calling the right to bear arms
A mirage between waves, Grey phantom sails
Sleeping Destiny, Born among whales
With honor, you fly red, white, and blue
Slip away into night. Godspeed be with you.

Chapter 7

On approach into Ruksan Air Base, South Korea, It takes a lot of extra power on the left throttles to keep the plane lined up. I ask my flight engineer, Macritt, what the EPR gauges (Engine Pressure Ratio) are doing. I am "crabbing", pointing diagonally from the runway, but at least able to track a straight line to it.

It is similar to if a crosswind is blowing us sideways, but I can see by the digital read-out on the INS (Inertial Navigation System), that there is no wind. If there was a crosswind, I would be using the controls to fly with my nose pointed into the wind, while my track over the ground stays where I need it, it's similar to steering a boat with a cross-current. It's a dark night over the Sea of Japan, and I scan the glowing engine instruments, but nothing is abnormal.

At times like this, you don't get scared, you just fly the plane. It takes all your concentration to deal with the situation, so there's a pleasant immunity from emotion. Macritt confirms, there is nothing wrong with our engines. Captain Bohan looks on without saying a word. He has more time in the lavatory of 747's, than I do at the controls. If I'm doing something wrong, I know he'll tell me. As the ship announces "10" feet above ground, I straighten out to land in line with the runway. I do so, and we land normally.

While taxiing in, I try to decipher the camouflaged netting over the machine gun pits between the taxiways. Who is in there aiming at me? I always wonder what those guys think about, lying in their gun emplacements all day and night.

Once parked on the ramp with the shutdown checklist complete, Bohan chuckles while looking rearward out his window. "Come look at this, Ava." A crowd of ground personnel is gathered under our left wing, with flashlights pointing straight up. One of our monstrous flaps is broken and hanging limply from the wing. No wonder I was being dragged sideways. One of our flaps is the size of a barn door, and normally only tilts to 25 degrees or less.

Our flap must have broken during its extension on approach. Interesting, and luckily not fatal during that slow phase of flight. Dangerous if we had to do a Go-Around. Deadly if it happens at high speed and high altitude. I love flying with Bohan. Once we were en route from a US Air Base in Japan, to one in Alaska. It was a rare weather day in Alaska, and I pointed out we were looking at Mount McKinley all the way from the coast. Without missing an opportunity, Bohan called Fairbanks Center, and requested "Direct Mount McKinley and Flight Level 210". We then circled the highest peak in North America, with a 747. It was my leg, so I hand flew around the summit while taking pics of Bohan with the peak behind him.

"This plane is hard broke. We're gonna be here for days unless they commercial us out. The golf course has the best SOS anywhere. Do you guys want to get brunch and play a round in the morning?" Bohan suggests, recommending the chipped beef on toast for brunch.

"Definitely" Macritt answers.

"You guys go ahead." I answer "I do love shit-on-a-shingle, but you know what GOLF stands for?" I sneak Bohan a teasing smile "Games Over Let's Fly."

"But actually", I continue seriously, "I have a couple of old friends based here and need to catch up with them."

We're interrupted by two familiar faces from way back. My friends Crack and Shag show up in the door of the cockpit. "What are you guys doing?" I yell to my old friends.

I explain to Bohan and Macritt, "I've known these guys many years because I grew up in Anapple Springs and they went to the Academy."

"How was your flight? It looks like you broke a flap" Shag's concerned.

"Ya, it must've been on approach when we extended it," I reply. "but that's nothing compared to a prop breaking off your Pitt's Special" I tease him about a mishap in our younger years. He handled that perfectly, of course, landing on a road. My old friends introduce themselves to Bohan and Macritt.

"What do you guys fly?" Bohan asks.

"F-16 sir" Crack answers sharply. He's 100% Texan and has been flying since he could reach the rudder pedals. Every year we meet up at the Reno Air Races. He's tall, slender, and the kind of friend that has your back. He's in a long-distance relationship.

"I'm on the A-10, sir" adds Shag, a California surfer with the sexiest voice ever. I used to lust after him. I surrendered those thoughts, the night he made me too many flaming Dr Pepper shots. He ended up helping me vomit on our friend's sidewalk. If only I could go back in time and drink less.

"Well, you young lads should come sit in our seats for a photo." Bohan offers.

"Thank you, sir," says Crack "We're shocked we came up here without being challenged. They're unloading Patriot missiles in the back, and we walked across the ramp and up your stairs wearing our civvies. We don't even have badges on, and no one noticed."

"Do we get to trade photo ops with you?" I suggest.

"Sure but it will have to wait. My squadron's having a Green Bean tonight, and I'm in charge of it" Crack answers.

"What's a Green Bean?" I ask.

"We have some new guys that just transferred in from The States, so we take them on a tour of America Village," Crack says, referring to the area just off base. "It's like an initiation, a tradition my squadron's been doing since the 1950's. You're coming with us, right?"

"Of course, just let me get my room key & change real fast," I reply.

"See you at the O-club in an hour." Shag and Crack take off.

Officer's clubs are more like sacred museums, than just eating and drinking establishments. They're packed with memorabilia from the history of every squadron ever based there. Behind every plaque, patch, and dinged-up airplane part, there's a harrowing story. It's steeped in nostalgic ambiance, as a symbol of unity and camaraderie. Each squadron has a colored t-shirt or scarf, a mascot, a saying, or even a movie that's quoted often. It's a momentary escape from the challenges of deployment.

I walk in to see a rowdy game of Crud happening, using "combat rules". Crud is a fast-paced game played on a pool table but without the sticks. It was invented by Canadian fighter pilots weathered in somewhere. A young guy in a bright red flight suit introduces himself at the bar. "What's your name?"

"Tess" I smile and shake his hand for effect "Tess Tickle"

He laughs hysterically, but admits "You have one hell of a grip."

"My dad flew Hellcats in World War Two and I learned three important things from him," I say, deciding to pass on the knowledge. "Give a firm handshake, always wear your shoulder harness, and nothing happens after midnight that doesn't happen before midnight."

"I think we could test out that last one" He winks "Later tonight I'm organizing a naked run down the runway. We just have to wait for the Tower to close." I like the way he thinks. I fantasize about gripping his flight suit zipper in my teeth and tugging it all the way down.

Unfortunately, Crack walks up to rescue me. "Hey, bugger off. She's with me. Are you ready, Ava?"

"Let's go" We walk off base with Shag and the three new guys. US air bases in other countries have a stain of humanity outside their gate. Poverty-stricken people have learned that GIs love booze and sex. Not necessarily in that order. As a result, there may be over a hundred bars within a mile of the main gate. In this town, 90% of them are crowded with topless women, called juicy girls.

Crack explains to his new guys, "The girls that work in the bars are selling drinks at an inflated price because what they're really selling is their companionship, and the offer of prostitution." He also explains as officers, they can buy the girls drinks but can get in trouble if they pay for sex.

"How do you know they are here by their own free will? Do you know if they keep some of the money they earn?" I ask him.

"I'm sure it's all on the up and up" Shag answers.

The party is just starting and I don't want to dampen the mood, so I bite my well-versed tongue.

Crack speaks up, "I do have a friend who says his regular Juicy, begged him to help her. She said she's locked up when she's not at the club. She was Filipino and didn't speak much English, so he was hoping he misunderstood her."

"Did he do anything about it?" I ask incredulously.

"He got transferred stateside. I'm not sure he told any of the higher-ups" Crack answers as we pile down some dirty stairs to a half-underground alley bar. Inside the Bogie House, we see glass bottles of liquor with dead, black snakes inside. I figure it can't be worse than the time I did a shot, from a cup with a frostbitten toe in it. That was in Yukon City, Canada, and they called it the Sourdough Toe. I flew my Pipe Cub on skis there for the weekend, to meet up with some Chinook pilots. They rode their snowmobiles in from 200 miles away because the road is closed in the winter. I thought the blackened toe was fake. It wasn't fake, and neither are these dead snakes.

"Here's to staying positive and testing negative" Shag toasts.

It doesn't taste bad, although I have no idea what sort of liquor the snakes are fermenting in. Crack announces that to receive a Bogie House t-shirt, we have to remove our shirts for a photo. I should've known by the polaroids on the wall. I feel thankful to be wearing a lacy, blue, sports bra because that's not coming off. Except for maybe on the runway run later tonight.

We put our shirts back on, layered with the new Bogie house shirts, and charge off to the next initiation spot, the Valhalla. It's packed with GIs and juicy girls. I've been to juicy bars enough that I'm not intimidated by all the other women being topless. I had to get used to it, because it's difficult to find a bar here that doesn't have juicy girls.

We secure a high-top table, and Crack approaches gingerly carrying an ammo bowl. It's a fruity, Soju cocktail in a ginormous bowl with 4 straws. Myself and the 3 FNG's are told we need to drink it all without stopping.

On the way to the next bar, we detour to an empty rooftop. We're about six stories up and Crack holds a bottle of the local Champagne, called Oscar. He reads a ceremonious speech dating back to when their squadron was formed. We all pass the bottle around until it's empty. Then to my shock, he throws it off the rooftop, we run down the stairs, and out into the street. I should've been a fighter pilot.

We rush a few streets over and duck into another go-go club, with pool tables overflowing with military men and juicy girls. "Next rounds on me" I turn and approach the bar. As a woman, I suspect I can buy drinks from the bartender directly, without paying for the topless girl that normally comes with it.

But I don't make it that far. The blood drains from my head as I recognize, Monique. I cannot believe my eyes. She is with other juicy girls, hanging onto young enlisted guys playing darts. I try to nonchalantly walk closer, to check for her beauty mark, and then I also see her emerald eyes. That's absolutely her.

I hurriedly return to Crack, "Do you see the Brazilian girl in the corner? She's underaged and was kidnapped. I know her family. I have to get her out of here."

Crack is solid. "What can I do?"

"Can you buy her a drink, and pretend you want to go to her room?" I plead, "We just need to get her to the street, and then we can run back to base with her."

"Then what? I'm risking my military career, and probably my entire career as a pilot" Crack presses his lips together, "Are you sure she was kidnapped?"

"100%" I affirm

"Where do we take her?" Crack continues, "We can't get her on base."

"Yes, we can." I take out my DoD card and press it into Crack's capable hands. "She and I both have tan skin and dark hair. Gate guards never question my DoD card, so she won't have to speak." My mouth dries and needles of fear shoot through my legs. I'm giving up my own safety and the protection of the air base. "If you can get her on base, I know some Navy SEALs that can get her out"

"She's half-naked" Jeffs's voice trails off, as he realizes what we're wearing.

I'm tracking the same thought, "I'll give her my Bogie House shirt. The gate guards will see you're all dressed alike, and they'll think she's me." I can tell by the look in Crack's eyes, he can get it done.

"Tell her you're taking her to her mother, Louisa, in Rio. It's pronounced with an H in Portuguese, so say it like 'He-oh'" I teach him. "I'll grab the guys and wait outside."

I look at Crack and hope I'm not ruining his life. The risk is high but if anyone can pull this off, I know these guys can.

"Call me when you get to your barracks room" I add.

Crack walks towards Monique and I talk to Shag and the new guys, trying to look calm in front of the bar cameras. "We have an emergency. We need to run the half mile back to base as quickly as possible. The juicy girl Crack is talking with is in danger. I gave her my DoD card. & I'm giving her my shirt too" I continue "You just need to pretend she is me. Can you guys please do that? You are literally saving her life."

They nod in shell-shocked agreement, and we head for the door to wait outside. I take off my Bogie House shirt as Crack appears, already running. Monique took her shoes off coming out the door and I cover her with my shirt. We run triumphantly through the dark streets, protected by my flyboy friends. This is one time I'm glad for the lack of streetlights. I'm impressed she's running as fast as me, but fear is a great motivator. Soon we see the stone arc of Ruksan's main gate in the distance.

We switch to a fast walk so as not to alert the gate guards.

"Monique" now, your name is "Ava," I tell her. Jeff hands her my ID card "Do you want to go home to Rio?" I ask.

"Yes," she replies in bursting floodgates of relief.

"We will help you. Stay with my friends." I'm not sure how much English she's learned while in captivity. I lift my index finger to my lips hoping she'll understand to stay quiet, and I break off into the shadow of an alley.

Watching from behind a corner, I unconsciously hold my breath as they approach the gate. Camouflaged among the guys, Monique walks right on base, just as I had onto the aircraft carrier. My heart is bursting with joy, but there's no time to revel in it.

My hotel is only a block away, and I've never run so fast in my life. I lock my door realizing I can't go out again until I have my DoD card back. I can't risk revenge from Monique's previous owner when he finds out his bottom bitch is gone. I'm trapped in this room until I can get on base. I consider what a small price to pay that is, compared with the places Monique has been trapped. I feel somewhat safe knowing my crew hotel is owned by an ex-Republic Of Korea soldier. Crack calls, "She's safe in my barracks apartment. Shag went to get her clothes and food from the commissary."

"Awesome." I exclaim "I will never be able to repay you enough. I'm calling my SEAL friends, to extradite her. Please have Shag bring my DoD card, so I can get on base after the gate guards' shift change. I'm probably not safe here."

"Absolutely. Shag said you can stay at his place" Crack answers. "Monique's English isn't great, and I can tell she's scared."

"Ok, see you soon" I hang up and call Steve.

He calls right back and It's so good to hear his voice "My friends and I will hop on MAC flights (Mobile Airlift Command). We'll see you tomorrow. Way to go, Ava, you are one determined woman."

"It's all right time, right place, and right friends" I answer. "It really just came together. What can I do to help? I'm going into days off, and I don't have a reason to go home."

"My buddy, and others from his non-profit, are taking Monique to Brazil. I'm just helping with contacts for the initial exfil." Steve explains. "I have a few days off. Do you want to climb Mount Fuji with me?"

"Absolutely." I happily respond, "It's only a two-hour flight to Japan."

"Alright, see you when I get there. Try to stay under the radar." Steve hangs up and I repack my things while waiting for Shag. I see my clipboard, with a copy of the flight plan still on it. Somewhere over the Pacific, I scrawled a poem on the back of it...

The turbulence competes with St Elmo's fire
For my attention
The view expands across my mind
With the Milky Way's ascension

My fingers slip down the windshield
And sparks fly to my hand
They dance along the airframe
With the wave of my command
A shallow attempt to connect with my world
The lights make me aware
A shock runs through my body
I find
I'm already there
Falling
As this fine rain
Then rime
On the flight controls
Hitching a ride through the electric mural
The cloud tapestry unrolls

A halo crowns the city
Soon to hear my engine's dirty song
South Korea is full of angels
Quiet, but not for long….

Inbound, my frivolous, foaming ambition
I ride a maze of igniters and nozzles
Inbound a mercenary of destruction
My engines scream, "Burn the fossils!"

And chokes, on it's own smoke
Pukes oil, and is sorry at least
Scraping metal parts unite
And there pounds the heart of my beast
Eye to eye, I'm grubby and sweaty
Hair balled in a rage
Shaking the ribs and spars
Of my metal coffin/cage
I can fly without this plane
These gages and needles drive me insane

A fist rushes out of cloud
Bouncing me where it wish
The wind pushes back, resisting
This damsel of distress

Scraping and clawing through the sky
Aircraft stumbles, barometer stalls
I have some weather in my pocket

Will I trip and fall?
Or settle a breeze,
And then no lift at all
"I have always been here"
The silence calls,
"And I am the wind that passes the storm"

Chapter 8

Three days later, on the train to Mount Fuji, Steve answers my questions about Monque's extradition. "There are 3,300 islands around Korea, many of them uninhabited. I helped my buddy procure a small boat, and during the night we delivered Monique to one of the atolls. A larger vessel took them out from there."

"What about the other juicy girls owned by that trafficking ring? Can your friends get them out also?" I ask hopefully.

"They already moved them. Possibly to areas around other military bases, or to brothels at nightclubs in tourist areas." Steve adds "A third of the tourists here are from Mainland China, and there are so-called love hotels marketed towards them."

"The US military has been here since the 1950's. Don't they take any responsibility for human trafficking?"

"The military knows that prostitution is out of control and they try to make it off limits. But they can't change it. Off-base means out of their jurisdiction. They have MPs patrolling and monitoring, but they can only arrest the GIs." Steve patiently explains "They can't do anything about foreigners owning women and pimping them out. The sex traffickers even see themselves as heroes for bringing money into impoverished areas."

That thought makes me squeamish. "But I thought prostitution was illegal in Korea."

"It is," Steve confirms "That's why it's harder to track and make sure women are working by their own free will, and keeping some earnings. The government can't regulate the business owners, because they're not paying taxes."

It's finally starting to sink in now. "That's why most of Europe, Australia, and even Nevada, made prostitution legal?" I ask.

"Yes, but sometimes it doesn't work. People find loopholes." Steve informs me. "Sex trafficking is still a problem in those places."

"I can totally see that." I agree "I met a hotel van driver in Australia, who accidentally was bragging about her 12 children. She was from India but had gained citizenship. I was asking her questions, thinking what a great mom she must be. But she eventually confessed, they weren't really her children. She adopts children from India so they can get citizenship, and then they import their parents. The parents must pay this woman a ton of money for that."

"My buddy had a message for you." Stave solemnly says, "He asked for you to keep an eye out in the airports. Traffickers are chartering entire planes, and moving kidnapped children to other countries en masse. If you see a lot of children and very few adults, it might not be a school field trip." Steve gives me a phone number to contact.

We transfer from the train to a bus and arrive at Mt Fuji's First Station. The hiking is relaxing and meditative. It feels like a spiritual pilgrimage and we enjoy the spring flowers. Above treeline, the climb is steeper. The switchbacks are lined with people sitting on boulders alongside the trail, smoking cigarettes. It's a cultural thing, half the World's smoking population lives in Asia. The terrain beneath our feet is round, porous, volcanic rocks, each about the diameter of a beer can. They roll like ball bearings under our feet. I realize the hike down is going to be treacherous and we don't have poles. Every couple hundred meters is a Tori or a shrine. High winds above us make layers of red and orange stratus, as the sunset turns the sky into a moving kaleidoscope of light.

We arrive at our refuge for the night. It's 8,800 ft above sea level, at the 7th station. The huts have boulders and old tires stacked on top of them, to hold down the roof when there's high wind. The sparse refuge offers dinner around rustic community tables. Copper tea kettles hang over open fires with stone chimneys. I can't read the signs on the walls because it's all in Japanese. We sit on pillows by a fire pit and warm ourselves. So far tonight we're the only English-speaking people here. It is traditional to spend the night at a hut, so the morning climb to 12,400' can be finished at dawn. It also gives you time to acclimate to the higher elevations.

We plan to awaken at 2 am and join the torch-lit parade to the summit for sunrise. "This is so much easier than Resurrection Pass." I appreciate, while slurping down some hot noodles. "Food, blankets, and real toilets. Instead of an outhouse buried in snow."

"Even better, the bunks here are wide enough for us to snuggle" Steve has that sparkle in his eyes, and a happy grin on his rough, unshaven face.

"You want to snuggle with me?" I shyly ask.

"Look at you pretending to be innocent. I've been waiting for this for months." I'm shocked by Steve's reply. I figured we were just going to be friends at this point. "It was a mistake to leave you in Amsterdam. I've been alone for a long time, and had given up on relationships." He looks at me smiling, "And you have to admit, you're a little intimidating."

"I can't help being me," I say wryly. "I know I come on a little strong for most people. I'm just high energy, and I'm decisive."

"You are decisive, and I love that about you. I'm glad you tracked me down." Steve says, completely serious now.

"Whenever I look at my watch, I remind myself I'm going to make time for you in my life."

I'm so elated seeing Steve look as happy as I feel. "I wasn't angry that you left in Amsterdam," I confess. "It's not my business what you do. My only business is to have as much fun as possible and see who shows up to join me." Steve holds me close, and I feel the stability and alignment of our synergy. It feels exciting, in a natural and easy way. A completeness I've never experienced.

Steve strokes my hair, kisses me, and says."You have an exceptional presence about you. I feel happy when I'm with you, and I want to spend a lot more time with you."

"Good, I think we'll have many adventures together" I smile and kiss him back tightly. Nightfall is blanketing us, and we snuggle intimately, wrapped in the mountain's solitude. The starry constellations flow across Fuji, like the poetry streaming through my mind's pages…

Walk thru a Tori
Bowing, enter your story
Of blossoming leaves
Dripping Sakura trees
Drawn in Mt Fuji's glory

Turning around
Heartbeat's passionate sound
In a Nihonga, I float
By the Tanka you wrote
Cherry petals surround

You're all that I see
Bedsheets envelope me
In rice paper moon
Stars falling soon
Paint me in mountains of Fuji

Samurai, all fear is gone
Akimbo swords drawn
Incandescent light
On summits height
Come, climbing at dawn

Printed in the United States
by Baker & Taylor Publisher Services